MES

Ans	_____	M.L.	_____
ASH	_____	MLW	_____
Bev	_____	Mt.Pl	_____
C.C.	_____	NLM	_____
C.P.	_____	Ott	_____
Dick	_____	PC	_____
DRZ	_____	PH	_____
ECH	_____	P.P.	_____
ECS	_____	Pion.P.	_____
Gar	_____	Q.A.	_____
GRM	_____	Riv	_____
GSP	_____	RPP	_____
G.V.	_____	Ross	_____
Har	_____	S.C.	_____
JPCP	_____	St.A.	_____
KEN	_____	St.J	_____
K.L.	_____	St.Joa	_____
K.M.	_____	St.M.	_____
L.H.	_____	Sgt	_____
LO	_____	T.H.	_____
Lyn	_____	TLLO	_____
L.V.	_____	T.M.	_____
McC	_____	T.T.	_____
McG	_____	Ven	_____
McQ	_____	Vets	_____
MIL	_____	VP	_____
	_____	Wat	_____
	_____	Wed	_____
	_____	WIL	_____
	_____	W.L.	_____
	_____		_____
	_____		_____
	_____		_____

THE PEBBLE BANK

Cara Karrivick and her twin sister never knew they had any family on their father's side. But when Cara and Arlene inherit their grandparents' cottage in Polmerrick, Cara visits the house and is delighted when she uncovers so many family secrets. She meets the rather hostile Josh Pellew, but it doesn't spoil her dream of living there. However, as Cara discovers her grandmother's family record, disaster strikes. Can Josh be the one to help her to realise her dream?

SHEILA SPENCER-SMITH

◆

THE PEBBLE BANK

Complete and Unabridged

LINFORD
Leicester

First published in Great Britain in 2007

First Linford Edition
published 2008

British Library CIP Data

Spencer-Smith, Sheila
    The pepple bank.—Large print ed.—
Linford romance library
    1. Family secrets—Fiction 2. Twins—Fiction
    3. Love stories 4. Large type books
    I. Title
    823.9'2 [F]

ISBN 978–1–84782–226–0

Published by
F. A. Thorpe (Publishing)
Anstey, Leicestershire

Set by Words & Graphics Ltd.
Anstey, Leicestershire
Printed and bound in Great Britain by
T. J. International Ltd., Padstow, Cornwall

This book is printed on acid-free paper

1

Cara hadn't expected Bal Cottage to be pink. Grey, yes, and as plain as its odd name, but not pink. Carefully she drove her car across the paved forecourt and drew up alongside the wall. On the other side of the road was the narrow arm of the harbour with a row of cottages on the high ground beyond.

This was it, Cara thought in wonder. Her late grandparents' old property.

She got out of the Fiesta and stood looking at the grey-tiled roof and knobbly walls of the cottage for a long considering moment. The windows on either side of the door gleamed back at her. Seagulls called somewhere in the distance and there was a pleasant whiff of salty tar in the air. Yes, great. Worth coming all this way to check up on their new possession, hers and her twin sister Arlene's, now that probate had been granted.

Smiling, Cara pushed back her long hair, yanked her travel bag out of the car and felt for the cottage key in the pocket of her jeans. She took a deep excited breath. The feeling of home-coming was as strong as if she had been coming here all her life instead of visiting Bal Cottage for the first time.

With a hand that trembled slightly she pushed the unwieldy key into the lock. It wouldn't fit. She tried again, fiddled it this way and that and then removed it. Come on, Cara, you idiot. What are you doing wrong?

They had received the key from the solicitor only last week in the padded envelope postmarked *Cornwall* and addressed to *Cara and Arlene Karrivick* at Arlene's home in Exeter. They already knew of their grandparents' legacy and Arlene had been ecstatic.

'Just at the right time,' she'd cried. 'We need money badly.' But when didn't she need money? Spendthrift Arlene, no surprise there. There was no question that the cottage must go on the market at once and Cara, at the moment unattached, had offered to go down and arrange it.

Cara had been visiting her sister at the time one of the two keys to the property arrived by special delivery. Arlene ripped the envelope open and started at the key in disgust.

'Look at the size of it,' she'd grumbled. 'Most likely for some old shack nobody would be seen dead in let alone want to spend thousands buying.'

But Bal Cottage wasn't an old shack. Not one of your roses and honeysuckle-round-the-door sort of cottages either. Just a stolid no-fuss building that looked as if it had been here for centuries staring out at the harbour and listening to the faint whine of machinery and the thump of something heavy being dumped nearby.

On either side of the cottage were buildings, a boathouse and what looked like a large storage shed. Not part of the property, thank goodness, Cara thought. The cottage would be quite enough for her to deal with.

Placing her bag at her feet, Cara weighed the key in her hand. She liked its heavy feel because it felt solid and safe. Or would do if she could get it to turn and open the door in front of her. She tried again. Still no good.

'Trouble?' said a voice behind her.

She spun round. The young man standing there in navy shorts and sweatshirt was looking at her with suspicion. Maybe he thought she was breaking in. He was holding his fishing rod as if it were a weapon.

'I can't get in,' she said. Obvious, of course, and humiliating that she couldn't even unlock the door of their own property. There was something about the way he was looking at her that made her want to justify her statement and she tried to turn the key again without success to prove what she said was true. 'They've given me the wrong key,' she added.

'They?'

'The solicitors.'

4

His eyes narrowed. 'And you are?'

What had that to do with anything? 'They sent the key,' she said, 'I'm visiting.'

'An empty cottage?'

She stared back at him. His dark hair was long and waved slightly. A lock of it fell across his forehead as he glanced up at the upstairs windows. He shook it back impatiently.

'An empty cottage,' she agreed. 'Apart from some furniture, of course, but I expect you know that.'

He turned and sent a frowning look in her direction. 'I do indeed. The place hasn't been lived in for months since the old man died.'

'I know that too.'

'But you haven't told me who you are.'

'Cara Karrivick, if that's any business of yours.'

A flicker of amusement lightened his features for a moment.

'You find that funny?'

His lips turned up at the corners. 'A

5

good Cornish name.'

'And?'

'And so. Karrivick.'

The way he said it sounded different from her pronunciation, but she made no comment. She pronounced her name with the accent on the first syllable and that was that. Too bad if he didn't like it. 'And you are?' she asked.

'Josh Pellew,' he said as if she should have heard of it. He moved his fishing rod from one hand to the other. 'Give me the key.'

Obviously her name passed some sort of test with him, however she chose to say it. She passed the key to him. His hands were large and his fingers long and tapered. She saw that the skin on ends of them was calloused as if he was used to gripping heavy objects.

'An old man lived here for the last year or two,' he said in such a forbidding tone she felt she was being judged in some way.

'My grandfather.'

He raised one eyebrow. 'Your grand-father?'

She made no reply, anxious now to get inside. She had left early this morning and the drive had seemed wearisome because of the heavy traffic and a long hold-up on the Bodmin bypass.

He frowned, hunching his shoulders. 'Come this way.'

Cara followed him to the back of the cottage and saw that the ground behind the building sloped up to a broken fence backed by the thick foliage of overgrown bushes. She could hardly see the ground for straggling brambles and stinging nettles. It looked neglected and forlorn.

She thought of her unknown grand-father living here after his wife died, not able to do much because of the weak state of his heart that eventually killed him. The front of the cottage had looked welcoming, but out here where the sun didn't reach she had a distinct feeling of sadness and decay.

Josh Pellew hesitated, still giving her a fierce scrutiny. She stared back, unwilling to let him know she found this disturbing. Then he fitted the key into the lock on the back door and pushed it open.

'There,' he said, standing back.

She went inside and turned to thank him, but he had gone. She wished she had explained how things really were, that until recently she and Arlene thought they had no family apart from Arlene's husband and her two young children. But what did it matter?

Josh Pellew was probably just a passer-by who despised her for her inadequacy. Given time she would surely have worked out for herself that there was another door for the key to fit.

She shrugged and put down her bag on the tiled floor of the large bare kitchen. The room was dim and smelt musty because of the sloping bank outside. The first thing to do was to open windows and get some fresh air into the place.

A wooden table stood in the centre, scratched and marked with some dark stains. Beneath the window was a deep porcelain sink with wooden draining boards on either side, none too clean.

There were no fitted units, but Cara saw a door on one wall that might lead to a larder. On the opposite wall was a framed painting of rocks and pebbles of all colours, shapes and sizes. Fascinating, but she had better explore the rest of the cottage before examining it more closely.

Apart from one next to the kitchen there was one other room downstairs. This seemed to have been used as a storeroom and Cara shut the door on it quickly. She would examine the contents later.

The room at the front looked over-furnished with shabby easy chairs and a round dining-table in one corner where strips of stained wallpaper hung loose. One wall was covered with a tall bookcase, spilling books. Upstairs were two bedrooms and the bathroom.

Cara stood at the window of the front bedroom and looked out at the narrow harbour with the line of cottages on the hill on the other side. But what caught her attention were the spars of the old sailing vessel tied up at the quay.

It was like an illustration in an old picture book she and Arlene had owned as children when they were living in Bristol. Their aunt and uncle who brought them up had seemed settled there for a while, but as usual their uncle's work meant moving once more to another place, one of the many of their childhood.

A flash of sunlight illuminated the tops of the masts. Cara clenched her hands at her side, wishing she'd brought her paints with her to do a quick watercolour sketch to remind her of how the scene felt. She could work it up later into an oil or acrylic. But useless to think of that now. There wouldn't be time for painting in the short time she was here. Sighing, she went downstairs again.

Later, having eaten the packed lunch she'd brought with her, Cara set to work. The large pieces of furniture were easy to list. Fortunately there weren't too many personal odds and ends though there must have been once. Maybe they had been packed away in the storeroom.

Piles of unread gardening magazines, newspapers and empty egg boxes she packed in some of the cardboard boxes she'd found stacked in the storeroom. These could be disposed of eventually when she could arrange transport. There were packing cases there too that might also be useful. Maybe Arlene could come down with her soon and they could do this together.

She found another, larger box and began to pile the books into it. On the top shelf, squeezed in between two large gardening books, she found a photograph album. Tempted to stop work for a moment, she carried it across to the settee.

Here was a find! She didn't know

who the people were, of course, but found the pages fascinating. She stopped at a full-page photograph of a young couple holding a small child. Her father? Incredible, but it must be. There were more photos of a growing child in the following pages and at last a wedding photo.

Cara stared at it with streaming eyes, knowing it must be her parents and wondering why she had never seen it before. There were no more of the son after that, only of her grandparents themselves, some taken on holiday and one of two in front of the cottage.

The last one of all must have been taken by the old man of his wife. She was standing in front of the bank in the garden. It wasn't overgrown then, but looked bright with a pattern of pebbles.

Cara snapped shut the album, unable to look any more, and replaced it on the shelf. When the box was full she left the rest of the books to be packed later and went to look at the inside of the front door. It was painted black like the outside.

She ran her fingers around the keyhole. There seemed no reason for the key not to be available. Perhaps it had got lost and never replaced. She must arrange to get another cut.

Not knowing if there would be bedding at the cottage she had packed a sleeping bag. She spread it out on the bed in the front room, liking the thought of waking up tomorrow to the view of the harbour and the sailing ship. She had already switched on the immersion heater for hot water for a shower. But now to take a look round outside.

She hadn't expected a beach to be so close, just down the road a little and bordered at one side by the harbour wall. A high cliff backed it and she scrunched over the pebbles to the rocks on the other side. It was so lovely here, the sea smooth and the headlands in the distance hazy against the pale sky.

She found a rock for a seat and sat

back, eyes closed, listening to the tiny ripple of waves and the seagulls' distant cries. The tangy scent of seaweed hung in the still air.

She thought of her grandparents living out their lives here in Polmerrick. She wished, suddenly, that she had known them, or at least known that she and Arlene had relations down here in Cornwall. Uncle Rob and Auntie Sadie had never mentioned them. How odd was that?

True, they were on the other side of the family, their dead father's side, but even so. Growing up, she and Arlene had never asked about his relations, assuming there weren't any.

Their own parents had died together in a road accident when the twins were little more than babies and their mother's sister and her husband had given them a home. Or homes, as it turned out, because they didn't stay in one place for long.

It was a wonder that they had ever learned anything at school, but Arlene had done well and she, Cara, could have gone to Art College except that Uncle Rob didn't approve. She had been so rebellious at first.

Anyway it was probably all for the best and she had enjoyed working in the flower shop her friend from school eventually started up in Exeter. Art lessons in the evening had been satisfying and later she had taken some day courses and even held a joint exhibition of her work with a fellow student. Strange that Arlene and family now lived in Exeter too now that the Met Office had transferred to a new headquarters there.

The rattle of disturbed pebbles made Cara sit up and open her eyes. For a moment she was dazzled by the brightness and then she saw that someone was walking across the pebbles towards the boat by the harbour wall. Josh Pellew. He had on a khaki-coloured jacket now and was carrying what looked like a couple of round cages. Lobster pots? Could be.

He must have seen her sitting over here on her rock, but he gave no sign. She had expected a wave of recognition at least. She picked up a stone and then dropped it again as she saw another she liked better. This one was round and smooth and had flecks of something shiny among the grey. It was obvious that he had ignored her deliberately.

She smoothed the stone in her hand, surprised at her hurt. Earlier he had helped her get in the cottage willingly enough even though he seemed to disapprove of her.

Josh Pellew dragged the boat down to the water's edge and pulled off his trainers. Then, pushing the boat out, he climbed aboard. The next moment the engine sprang to life and he was away.

She watched him go, his wake disturbing the quiet sea, until he was out of sight behind the harbour wall. Slipping the pebble in the pocket of her jeans, she stood up. He had seemed to be familiar with the cottage and had known that the key was for the back door.

He knew her grandfather, probably her grandmother too, before she died.

Cara walked across the beach deep in thought. Instead of going indoors she walked straight past, wanting to see what else Polmerrick had to offer. Driving down the road in the taxi this morning, intent on her first glimpse of the cottage, she had been oblivious of anything else.

Now she saw that further up were one or two shops, a mini store and a post office, a shop selling holiday things and an estate agent. The name above the door surprised her. *A. J. Pellew*. Josh had sounded as if he expected his name to have meant something to her and this was obviously why.

She looked in the window. There were plenty of houses for sale in the district, but nothing in Polmerrick. The lack of competition could be a good thing for Bal Cottage when it went on the market. At one side of the window a large plan of a new holiday complex took up most of the space. On the other was an advertisement for a cleaner, six mornings a week.

Maybe it would be a good plan to employ someone to clean Bal Cottage when it was ready to go on the market. There was much to do before then, of course, but it would speed things up.

Cara pushed open the door and went in. The woman behind the desk looked up with a smile. 'Are you looking for anything in particular, m'dear?'

'Well, no,' Cara admitted. 'I'd like to make enquires about putting a property on the market.'

'I see. Then please take a seat and I'll take a few details.'

'I just need to talk to someone and find out how it's done. I'm only here till tomorrow and the cottage isn't ready yet.' Cara knew she sounded as if she didn't know what she was doing, but she couldn't help it. The cottage seemed to be pulling at her in a way she couldn't explain.

The person on the other side of the desk smiled pleasantly as she smoothed her grey hair behind her ears. Her pink cardigan was buttoned up to her neck and she had pearl earrings that caught the light from the window as she moved her head. 'I think you should talk to Mr Pellew,' she said at last. 'He's out at the moment showing someone round a property, but he'll be back in about half-an-hour if you'd like to call back. He'll tell you when he can do a viewing to give an estimate.'

'But I won't be here after tomorrow.'

'That's no problem, m'dear. You'll be able to leave us a key when you go?'

'A key?'

'That's the usual way if the vendor is not available.'

'I'll think about it,' Cara said. She fingered the key in her pocket, strangely reluctantly, suddenly, to commit herself.

2

Arlene and Tom lived on the outskirts of Exeter with their two young children a couple of miles away from her own small flat. Cara negotiated the round-about near Sainsbury's, drove up the road past the church and then slowed down to turn right into a cul-de-sac of terraced white houses.

Parking her car in one of the allotted parking spaces for the end house she leapt out, anxious to tell her sister what she felt about the pink cottage down in Cornwall. It was only a few days since she was last here and yet how different she felt now about the property she had gone to see in the village of Polmerrick that already felt like home.

Smiling, Cara smoothed her navy shirt down over her slim hips. A few steps and she'd reached the front door. She paused in surprise. Had she come to the wrong house? But no, there was the number six on the door beneath the fancy glass panel of trellis and red roses that definitely hadn't been there before.

'A new door?' Cara said as it opened to reveal Arlene smiling at her with young Jamie clutching her long flowing skirt and three-year-old Minda behind him.

Arlene swung Jamie into her arms. 'Like it?'

'It's different.'

'They fitted it yesterday. Lends a touch of class, don't you think? And it should do, the price it cost. But come on in. It's not the only new thing we've got to show you.'

Cara bent down to give Minda a hug and a kiss, and then holding her hand followed Arlene through the small entrance porch into the room that stretched to the open patio doors at the end. Here the room narrowed to allow room for the kitchen area on the right. On Friday the kitchen floor had been of orange vinyl tiles. Now, three days later, they had all been ripped up.

Arlene laughed and pushed her brown hair behind her ears, something Cara often did herself. They weren't identical twins, she and Arlene, but they had this gesture in common.

'The kitchen floor had to be levelled properly before the ceramic tiles go down,' Arlene said, her eyes sparkling. 'They're going to be blue and white speckled. I can't wait for them to get started. We're out in the garden, so come through.'

The large paved area outside was scattered with toys. Cara sat down on a low cushioned chair and Arlene moved a pile of catalogues off another for herself. Jamie was soon occupied with a wooden train and Minda with two teddy bears dressed alike in tartan and shirts Cara hadn't seen before.

'So,' said Arlene, leaning back. 'What was the place like?'

Cara took a deep breath. There was so much to tell and her words spilled out as she tried to infect her sister with the same enthusiasm for Bal Cottage and Polmerrick as she felt herself. But Arlene's expression deepened into impatience as Cara finished describing the cottage and told of the old sailing vessel berthed in the narrow harbour and the way the waves churned the pebbles on the beach and the bracing saltiness in the air.

'But what's the condition of the place? Did you do anything about getting it on the market?'

Cara shook her head. 'It's too soon. I started on the clearing up, but it's in a poor state.' She took the teddy bear that Minda brought to her and smoothed his bright trousers. 'I think we should keep the cottage, Arlene. It would be a wonderful place for holidays when it's cleaned up a bit.'

Arlene look surprised. 'You think so? But doesn't it rain a lot down there?'

Cara shook her head, laughing. 'Our grandparents lived there. They were family, and we're lacking in family roots since Sadie died. You ought to see their old home for yourself. The children would love the beach.'

Arlene glanced down at the catalogues at her feet. 'Is the furniture any good?'

'Only fit for the tip, I think,' Cara said sadly. 'Once it would have been cared for and loved, but now it's so decrepit there's nothing else for it. The wallpaper's peeling off in places, too. It's in a poor state.'

'It'll cost a lot to do up,' Arlene said. 'Tom won't like it. He says I spend too much.'

Cara leaned back in her seat. Now that she was away from Bal Cottage she felt as if invisible cords were pulling her back. A vision of Josh Pellew scrunching across the beach with his lobster pots shot into her mind and she had such a strong feeling of homesickness she almost gasped.

'The cottage wasn't lived in for months,' she said. 'I think the old man, our grandfather, couldn't do much before he died and let things go.'

'All the more reason for selling it.' Arlene bent to pick up one of the catalogues. She flipped it open to a page featuring colourful three-piece suites. 'Trust us to get lumbered with a place like that instead of some neat and tidy little property that would fetch a good price. They couldn't even spell its name properly,' she added in disgust.

Cara smiled. 'There's probably a reason for that.' She had wondered about the odd name, too, but then thought that it added to the attractiveness of the place. She liked it. 'I've got leave owing,' she added. 'I'll arrange to take it and go down there again. Three weeks. I could do a lot at Bal Cottage in three weeks. I'll find out where the local tip is and get rid of a lot of stuff. You know what they say, make the place look as good as you can. Get rid of the clutter. Sell a lifestyle.'

'It would look a lot better, I suppose.'

Cara handed the teddy bear back to his loving owner. The idea of spending her holiday in Polmerrick had come to her suddenly and she felt light-hearted and confident. Now that Mike was no longer on the scene she needed a project like this to concentrate on. Next stop the flower shop.

She knew that the new owner of *Flower Power* would be pleased to have her out of the way on holiday and there was nowhere she would rather be then Polmerrick. The owner had dropped enough hints about ex-colleagues keen to work there that there should be no problem with cover. Or even with her job itself.

With Bal Cottage and Polmerrick to think about she simply didn't care. Maybe when Arlene saw how good Bal Cottage looked she'd change her mind about wanting to sell it.

* * *

On Friday evening Cara shut the door of her Exeter flat behind her with a feeling of anticipation. Her car was piled high with cleaning things including her vacuum cleaner as well as enough clothes and belongings to last three weeks. She also had an insulated bag stuffed with the contents of her store cupboard and fridge and all her painting gear. As well she had packed her iron and small ironing board.

She had delayed her start to ensure a fairly traffic-free drive down to Cornwall and made good time. Dusk was beginning to fall as she drove down Polmerrick's broad street to the harbour, dimming the view of masts and spars of the old sailing ship still berthed there. Lights glimmered from the cottages high up on the opposite side.

This time there was no problem about getting inside Bal Cottage. Cara unloaded the car and then pulled the curtains across the cottage windows and set about making coffee. The warmth from the electric fire, when she switched it on, was welcome in spite of the smell of dust that rose from it. In artificial light the place looked homely and she had three whole weeks to make it shine before its future was settled.

Tonight she felt hopeful that Arlene would come to see it as she did herself, a place where they had roots and could feel they belonged.

In the light of day her spirits dropped. There was much to do and even when the place was tidied up and cleaned money would have to be spent on bringing it up to modern-day standards. But she could make a start on the kitchen as soon as she had eaten something.

Breakfast was bread and marmalade and coffee made with the last of the milk she had brought with her. She found a battered tin tray and carried everything outside. She ate, perched on the retaining wall that held back the overgrown bank. Later she would make a start on the brambles and stinging nettles.

The sun was rising above the high ground on the other side of the harbour and all at once the air felt warmer even though she was still in shadow. It was going to be a beautiful day. She would start by getting the curtains down and soaking them in turn in the sink while she started on the storeroom and made a pile of rubbish and unwanted items out here in the garden.

★   ★   ★

A hidden bell jangled somewhere behind the inner door of the mini-market as Cara pushed open the outside one and went inside. She picked up a basket and pulled a list from her pocket.

'Oh my dear life!' someone exclaimed coming round the end of the high shelves. 'You fair startled me.'

Not knowing that anyone was there Cara was surprised too. She smiled at the woman she had seen in the estate agent's when she was down last. It was good to see a familiar face.

'Ellie Trevean,' the woman said, beaming back at her. 'Doing a shop are you?'

'Just a few things I need,' Cara said, taking a jar of coffee from the shelf and putting it in her basket. 'I'm Cara Karrivick.'

'Josh said.'

'He did?'

'Such a nice boy, Josh. Ah yes, m'dear, I've known him since he was a little lad coming to me for his croust. Always hungry, he was, in them days and me ready to spoil him with nice warm split. Ah yes, poor boy. Such a bad shock to him when he didn't get the place after all. Promised it to him, it was, too. But he took it well, I'll say that for him.'

Cara smiled though it seemed as if Ellie Trevean was speaking a different language. She couldn't begin to imagine what she was talking about in her soft Cornish burr.

Ellie put a jar of coffee in her basket, too, and gave a deep sigh. She was wearing a hand-knitted mauve cardigan today, buttoned to the neck. 'I just ran out the office for a moment for this and some milk,' she said as she moved along.

Cara nodded, trying to imagine the stout Ellie running anywhere in the high-heeled shoes she was wearing. Her broad face looked slightly flushed, and no wonder. Cara's lips twitched. 'I'm here for three weeks,' she said, feeling she should give some sort of explanation. 'Doing a bit of tidying of the cottage. There's a lot needs doing.'

'A good clean as like as not,' Ellie agreed, her eyes brightening. 'We could do with a good cleaner at our place.'

Cara laughed. 'When I've finished with Bal Cottage I'll be shattered. Did you know my grandparents?'

'Your grandmother was a sweet old lady,' said Ellie, reaching for a packet of Bourbons. 'Good, they've had these in, Josh's favourites. He'd be telling me off a treat if I came back without them.' Her face crinkled into a smile. 'Josh used to tell me a lot about your grandad. He saw a lot of him after your grandma died. He kept himself to

31

himself then. A very fine old man. Very proud. Stubborn too, but I shouldn't be telling you that, should I?'

'I'm glad to know anything about him,' said Cara wistfully. Later she would get the photograph album down again and go through it again.

'Josh will tell you. Ask him, m'dear.'

Involuntarily Cara took a step back. She hoped that the expression on her face didn't tell Ellie of her dislike of the beloved Josh.

Ellie had finished her shopping now and was about to move to the till. 'You want to talk to them at the museum too, m'dear. Your grandad liked to help out there before he got too ill. It's over the other side of the harbour, back a bit. They'd be able to tell you a bit more than me.'

'Thanks I'll do that later on,' said Cara. 'But first I need to ask someone where the nearest tip is.'

'Easy, m'dear. Just up the road and turn right at the roundabout. You'll see a sign to it on your left. You can't miss it.'

'That's my next job.'

'Pop in, why don't you, when you've done? Have a word with Mr Pellew, Mark that is. There's always a cup of coffee for my favourite clients, and any friend of Josh's is a friend of mine.'

Cara opened her mouth to deny any friendship between them, but then closed it again and smiled her thanks. She finished her shopping, paid the elderly man at the cash desk and went back to Bal Cottage.

By the time she'd loaded four bulging bin bags and a lot of loose stuff into her car she felt exhausted. And dirty too, after such an orgy of clearing out the storeroom. There was a hole in her jeans below the knee where she'd caught her leg against something and a massive black splodge on the left of her T-Shirt. Never mind. She wasn't exactly going anywhere that needed dressing up.

Smiling, she got into the car. Ellie Trevean's directions were fine as far as the entrance to the amenity site, but she hadn't said that it was a narrow one and that there was very little room to turn inside. Cara sat in a long queue of cars similarly loaded, waiting for the ones at the front to manoeuvre their way out again. The sun was warm on her left cheek and her hair had come loose from its rubber band. She pushed it back behind her ears.

Gradually she moved forward until it was her turn to unload. The household item skip was clearly marked. She yanked the first bag out and heaved it up the steps to empty out. This was the heaviest. The other three were easier to deal with and she wiped her hand across her moist forehead when she had disposed of the contents of the last one. Exhausting work and she had almost had enough.

Back in the car again, she put the car into reverse and moved back. A shuddering thump jolted her to a stop. For a second she sat there and then became aware, suddenly, of someone close by. The irate driver of the car behind . . . Josh Pellew. This was all she needed. She got out of the car.

'What d'you think you're playing at?' he demanded, his voice hoarse.

'You gave me no room.'

'Room? There's masses of room.' He waved his arm to demonstrate, but she was unconvinced.

She looked at the front of his Mondeo hard against the rear of hers. 'I'll move forward.'

'You better had. You're holding everything up.'

She moved forward and got out again. 'No damage,' she said in relief.

'No thanks to you. D'you want me to get you out.'

'I do not.' She rammed the gear lever into reverse. The cheek of the man.

This time she was more careful. Conscious of his scrutiny she was determined to do the job properly and she inched slowly round until she had a clear way out. He got back in to his vehicle prepared to move.

He wound down his window as she

drew level. 'I saw you ditching all those bags,' he said.

'So I was.'

His eyes narrowed. 'Important stuff? I hope you know what you're doing.'

'For goodness sake!' What did he imagine she was destroying? And what business was it of his anyway?

She moved her foot on the accelerator as impatient hooting came from one of the other cars. 'Just leave me alone,' she cried. She hadn't queried the rubbish he was tipping here and in fact didn't care what it was. So why was he so interested in hers?

★ ★ ★

After a simple lunch eaten at the freshly-scrubbed wooden table in the kitchen, Cara decided to tackle the overgrown bank at the back of the cottage. She was pleased with her morning's work even though it had resulted in the unpleasant meeting with Josh at the amenity tip.

She was still seething at his attitude towards her, but she wouldn't think of that any more.

She donned a large pair of shabby gardening gloves she found in the cupboard in the storeroom, so ancient and stiff the fingers wouldn't bend, and set to work. Soon she had a pile of brambles and stinging nettles. If she went on like this another trip to the amenity site would be indicated. But oh no, not if Josh was there again keeping a close watch on what she was up to.

She yanked up a handful of long grass, surprised that the roots came up easily. Then she saw why. Underneath was an area of pebbles laid out in some sort of order. She pulled up more weeds, suddenly interested. More rounded stones were revealed until she saw that the pattern stretched right across from one side of the garden to the other. Many were missing, but there were enough left to show the intention. It looked as though some-one had placed them deliberately to form the shape of a vortex.

Cara sat back on her heels, thinking hard. Had her grandparents made this so many years ago that time and weather had damaged the pattern? It would seem like it. She felt a glow of warmth spread through her. This was a link with the past. A precious link. Someone in Polmerrick might know of it and be able to tell her.

3

Cara found the museum tucked away behind some more imposing buildings at the top end of the harbour.

She pushed open the door and went into the small reception area.

'Bal Cottage?' the curator said in faintly belligerent tones when she asked about it, looking at Cara with interest. He was a tall man, slightly stooped, the thinning hair on his head still retaining the hint of red in it that must have once made him stand out from the crowd. Eric Trubshaw was the name on his desk and seemed to suit him so well that Cara smiled.

'I'm told that you knew my grandfather,' she said.

'Jack Karrivick?' he said. 'Helped out here on and off for a good few years. A wise man, Jack. Got on well with the visitors, especially the young children.'

'I didn't know him, you see, or my grandmother.'

She was glad he made no comment about that though he must have wondered. Instead he punched a machine on the desk and issued her with a ticket, waving away her attempt to pay for it. 'I don't know what the name of their cottage means either,' she said.

'Bal Cottage?' he said. 'Easy, that one. They called the women who worked down the tin mines, bal maidens. We've a room through here dealing with all that. You'll see in a minute. Aye, bal maidens they were.'

'I see,' said Cara, though she didn't really. Maybe some of the previous tenants, before her grandparents bought the cottage, had worked in the mines. It didn't tell her anything about her grandparents though.

Eric Trubshaw seemed to guess what was in her mind. 'It's shipwrecks your grandfather was interested in,' he said. 'The shipwreck exhibition's through there. You'll have seen some of the bigger pieces of wrecked boats out in the yard as you came in. Aye, he was knowledgeable, your grandad. There wasn't much he didn't know about the Wreckers.'

'Wreckers?'

'Aye, the Wreckers. You'll have heard of men luring ships on to the rocks. Valuable cargoes, some of them. You'll have seen the book Jack wrote on the subject?'

She shook her head. There was so much she didn't know. Could be she'd find a copy among the books she hadn't yet examined? She'd look as soon as she got back. Meanwhile she'd come up with as many questions she could think of as she wandered around. The curator, Eric Trubshaw, might be able to answer them at the end if he wasn't too busy.

She started with the shipwreck exhibition, which filled two rooms. Interested as she was, because of her grandfather's interest, she found her mind wandering. When had her grand-parents first come to live in Polmerrick and how was it that contact between them had been lost?

Aunt Sadie had never mentioned them, perhaps wanting to keep the twins to herself with no interference from their father's side of the family. But what had she denied them, she and Arlene, as they were growing up? Cara moved on to the second room, feeling a flicker of resentment that wouldn't quite go away.

Immediately her interest quickened as she saw that here was an exhibition of recent work being done in the recording of old wrecks in this area, a fairly new thing, apparently. So many old wrecks had been virtually forgotten until this work began. Computer technology was a tremendous help here, of course.

She saw underwater photographs with clearly-typed explanations of what was being accomplished and how. There were photos of artefacts washed up on beaches after storms. She looked closely at a coloured photograph of a group of men standing on the beach she recognised examining a large piece of blackened timber. Surely that was Josh among them? She would know that mop of dark hair anywhere? Thoughtfully she moved on to the next stand.

By the time she had given the rest of the exhibits in the museum a cursory glance she was ready with the things she most wanted to know.

Eric Trubshaw smiled as she approached and shuffled some papers on his desk as he stood up. 'Jack would come in to help once or twice a week,' he said, 'Very kind and reliable, he was, always. Did whatever I asked him without grumbling like the chap we had before. Jack couldn't come in so much in the latter days when he was growing weak. Withdrawn, too, and not wanting to leave the cottage so much. The young chap, Josh Pellew, saw more of him then. He'd often call round of an evening for a bit of a chat.'

'You don't know what they talked about?'

'Wrecks most likely. Very knowledge-able, your grandad. Josh appreciated that. It was Josh who found him slumped on the kitchen floor that last time. Oh yes, Jack relied on Josh a good bit at the end.'

Cara cleared her throat. 'But before that, when he first came to work here?'

Eric Trubshaw busied himself issuing tickets to a family who came in at that moment. A little bit of fuss when the toddler demanded an ice-cream and then shrieked when thwarted. At last he turned back to Cara.

He pulled forward a chair. 'Sit down, m'dear.' He seated himself behind his desk and leaned on it, one hand beneath his chin. The sunlight from a small window above highlighted the red strands in his hair.

She listened, fascinated, to all he could tell her from the time Jack and Marion Karrivick had moved into Bal Cottage twenty-five years before when he himself was a young man and hadn't known them well, to the last years when he hadn't seen so much of her grandfather as he had when he first came to work at the museum.

He told of Jack's joy when his book was published and how it sold well locally and how his wife, Marion, had made sure it had pride of place in their own front room for many years. But there still seemed so much missing that Cara would have liked to know.

Grandchildren were never mentioned and he knew nothing of the pebble vortex she had discovered beneath the encroaching brambles.

★ ★ ★

That evening, Cara had another go at the brambles and stinging nettles, hacking them down with a scythe she found beneath the sink in the kitchen and yanking up the roots when they were not too difficult to get out.

By the time she heard the rabble of

the side gate opening and swung round to see who had come through into the back garden, she had cleared a good space and could see more of the pebble pattern beneath.

She might have known her visitor was Josh Pellew. Who else would it be shutting the gate behind him and coming forward so confidently as if he owned the place? Her heart lifted a little to see him though she still felt sore at his interfering comments at the amenity site.

'No sense hammering on the front door,' Josh said. 'You'll have to get a key cut.'

'All in good time,' Cara said tartly, sitting back on her heels.

He looked round at the overgrown garden and his eyes narrowed as he saw the work she was doing. 'You've been busy here.'

Cara struggled to her feet, brushing earth from her jeans. 'Did you want something or is this just a friendly call?'

He seemed to miss the irony in her

words. 'You know what you're doing, I hope?'

'As well as the next person.'

'I used to come in and lend your grandfather a hand about the place sometimes.'

She scratched the red itchy patch on the back of her wrist that the stinging nettles had caught. 'You did? But you didn't make much of a job of this, did you?'

Josh frowned. 'I'm not sure you should be hacking it in this way.'

'An expert then, are you?'

He knelt down on the damp patch she had cleared and touched the stones, running his hands over them as if he could discern a meaning in the pattern.

The back of his neck above his blue T-shirt looked vulnerable and for a moment she wanted to touch it. Then he straightened and sat back on his heels looking up at her in deep suspicion.

'All I'm doing in cutting back these brambles,' she said, annoyed at being on the defensive. 'And dealing with the stinging nettles as you can see.'

'But disturbing the roots could ruin this pattern.'

'And would it matter?'

He made no reply, but patted a few of the pebbles into place. She found his silence disturbing and moved further away from him. 'It looks as if it's meant to be a vortex shape,' he muttered.

'Somebody made it long ago,' she said, wishing she'd had time to clear more of the undergrowth. 'No-one seems to know why it was done. Not that I've spoken to many people in Polmerrick. Ellie Trevean, Eric Trub-shaw . . . '

He shrugged. 'He wouldn't show anybody, your grandfather. I wanted to clear this bank, but he wouldn't let me touch it.'

'Showed a bit of sense, then, didn't he?' Cara said. She placed the scythe on the ground by the fence, removed the clumsy gardening gloves and threw them down beside them. 'You haven't said what you came for.'

He glanced at her in surprise as he stood up. 'Ah yes, I nearly forgot. An apology. I got side-tracked when I saw this.' He waved his hand. 'Why did Jack want to keep it a secret? I respected his wishes, of course, about leaving the garden as it was. After all, I could have had a go at it when it was mine. There was no hurry.'

'Yours?'

'Mine. Bal Cottage is rightfully mine.'

Cara couldn't speak for a moment for surprise and indignation. He seemed sane enough as he stood in the shadow of the cottage looking thoughtfully at the pattern of pebbles she had unearthed so far, but this was an astounding thing to come out with. 'What do you mean, yours?'

'Jack often said he wanted me to have Bal Cottage when he'd gone. I was fond of him, you know, and he of me.'

Stunned at his tone of arrogant confidence, she gazed back at him. 'But that can't be true. He left it to my sister and me, his grandchildren. His solicitor . . . '

'But that's not the issue of the moment.' Josh looked at her keenly for a moment. 'I came to apologise to you. I was concerned that you were throwing out things of sentimental value to Jack without realising. His solicitor sorted through his papers, of course, and I was with him. But there are other things . . . his books, photo album . . . '

'All quite safe,' she said, tight-lipped.

Josh nodded. 'I was out of order at the tip.'

'But not as much as you are now,' Cara said, her voice crisp. 'It's completely legal, our ownership, Arlene's and mine. I can assure you of that. It's ours.'

'But morally mine, I think,' he said.

Cara opened her mouth to retort that he was wrong, but he was gone, closing the garden door behind him. She looked after him in amazed disbelief. Had she dreamed this or had he really been standing there, saying that the cottage was his? His statement was ridiculous.

The solicitor wouldn't have made an important error like that. They had seen a copy of the will. There was no mistake. Had there been a later will it would no doubt have been discovered. Josh himself would have seen to that.

It was impossible to work out here any longer after such a revelation. Her emotions in turmoil, Cara left everything as it was, grabbed her jacket and locked the back door behind her. She needed to feel the sea air on her face, to feel the salty breeze in her hair. Josh's assertion had been a shock.

Hardly thinking what she was doing, Cara ran down the road alongside the harbour and crossed the narrow bridge over the lock gate at the entrance to the narrow harbour. Here was an area of concrete with a small round building at the end. This was the harbour master's office marked by the brass plate on the wall.

From here there was a fine view of the coastline on either side and she saw another beach here that she hadn't discovered before, obviously more popular than the other. This one, backed by the high cliffs was larger than the one on her side of the harbour, with sand near the water's edge. There were rock pools too. Out to sea some sailing dinghies moved leisurely on the calm water.

Cara watched them for a few moments and then turned to look at the row of cottages behind her and then across to the buildings on the other side. Bal Cottage, with its pink walls and thatched roof, looked small compared to the sheds and warehouses that bounded it on either side. It looked comfortable, though, as if it had been there for ever.

After a while, Cara saw that there were steep steps leading down from the wall. Halfway down there was another way to the beach in the form of a short tunnel through the wall. She waited for a father and young son to come up the steps, talking loudly, and then went down herself.

At the bottom she saw someone waving to her among a group of children. Ellie Trevean, not wearing her fluffy cardigan today, but clad in neat shorts and flowery blouse and looking as if her white limbs hadn't been exposed to the sun very often. She waved back.

'Nice down here, isn't it?' Ellie called to her. 'Come down for a swim?'

'Just exploring,' Cara said, smiling. 'Researching suitable scenes for my painting.' Now what had made her say that? But it could be true if she was in Polmerrick long enough to set to work.

The area positively demanded to be portrayed on canvas.

Ellie smiled. 'You paint? How lovely. So much talent to be able to do that, m'dear. All I'm fit for is a spot of childminding. My sister's tribe, you know.' She looked at her charges proudly, obviously enjoying herself. 'You must let me see your paintings one day.'

'I will,' Cara promised, moving on.

Over at the other side, the cliffs curved to form an arm that stretched out into a rocky promontory covered in seaweed. There were fewer people here and Cara sat down on a handy boulder to view the scene critically. She liked the shape the huge rocks made with the cliff behind with the gulls wheeling above. There was plenty here to keep her brushes busy for weeks.

Suddenly she longed to portray her growing love for Polmerrick in the way she knew best. She picked up a pebble and lobbed it into a pool, watching the widening circles on the clear water. Her painting gear was always with her, packed away in the boot of the car. She would bring it down here one evening and set to work.

Suddenly she knew that she didn't want to leave when her three weeks were up. Just now she had told Ellie Trevean of her plans to paint and Ellie hadn't mentioned her original intention of putting Bal Cottage on the market, assuming, no doubt, that Cara had changed her mind.

The season was just beginning and there were advertisements in the post office window for seasonal jobs . . . cleaning holiday properties, for instance, working in the craft shop next to Pellew's. Why not? *Flower Power* would let her go without a murmur, anxious to get some of their own people in. No problem there.

A shudder of anticipation ran through her, drowning her apprehension at Josh's odd assertion about the ownership of the cottage. She was aware that what he said had strengthened her resolve to do everything in her power to stay and to think seriously about her future.

But there was Arlene to consider.

Cara reached for another pebble and examined it closely as if it could tell her what she needed to do. She knew she must talk to Arlene. She needed to share the knowledge that someone else thought he had a right to the place. In her head she seemed to hear her sister's voice . . . his word only. What proof could he produce that he wouldn't have done already if what he said was true? None, obviously. A load of nonsense that no-one would fall for.

Well, yes, but Josh had sounded so sure. Arlene should come down to Polmerrick and see Bal Cottage for herself. Once she had done that she might well fall in love with it too. And if Arlene agreed with her that the best plan was to keep the cottage in the family for holidays there would be no problem.

Meanwhile she could get a job locally, live in the cottage and pay rent to Arlene. This would give her the opportunity to work hard at her paintings and perhaps start a profitable career. She had plenty of inspiration she needed on the doorstep.

If Arlene agreed.

4

By the time Cara got back to Bal Cottage she had changed her mind about phoning Arlene immediately. Better to wait until she'd checked with the solicitor that all was in order and they were the legal owners. She had no doubt of course, whatever Josh Pellew said, but it would be good to be certain.

Instead, she got her painting gear out of the car, carried it into the kitchen and plonked it on the table. It was great seeing it all again, fingering the tubes of oil and acrylic paint and lining up her brushes in order of size just for the fun of it.

All this was now ready for the first opportunity to use it. With luck it wouldn't be long. She smiled as she humped up the bag and placed it ready in the hallway.

Then she went outside in the dusk to

gather up the scythe and gardening gloves from where she had left them. The air was balmy and still there was a faint hint of colour in the sky above the hillside to the west.

Feeling a surge of optimism, Cara smiled as she went indoors again and locked the door behind her. The future had taken on new meaning. There was purpose in her life, not only to find more out about Jack and Marion Karrivick, her unknown grandparents, but also make a life for herself that involved her first love, painting.

Her dreams that night were filled with colour . . . of the sea and of the sky and of the seaweedy rocks. A feeling of happiness pervaded over all that somehow was tied up with the pebble vortex in the back garden. It was a pattern that could go on for ever, growing and growing.

She awoke smiling, saw it was early and got up at once, anxious to find the book her grandfather had written about Cornish shipwrecks. In her excitement last night about staying on for a few weeks she had forgotten about this. The book was thinner than she had imagined, tucked between two larger volumes on the bottom shelf of the bookshelves in the front room.

She pulled it out with trembling fingers and carried it into the kitchen and opened the flyleaf. She looked at the title and the author's name with a glow of pride. *Cornish Wreckers by Jack Karrivick*. This was her grandfather and it was a thrill to see it.

Savouring the moment, she filled the kettle at the sink and plugged it in to make coffee. While it was cooling she seated herself on one of the rickety wooden chairs at the table and began to read.

Jack had a way with words that made the scenes he described spring to life. In her mind's eye she saw the lines of men going secretly down the paths from the cliff tops to gather in cargoes washed ashore from the broken ships on the rocks.

She read, enthralled, until she reached the last page. A lot of research had gone into this, she thought. No wonder he and her grandmother were so proud. She was too. She couldn't wait to show Arlene.

She glanced at her watch. Time for a leisurely breakfast here at the table and another glance through the book she could hardly bear to put down.

The solicitor's number was in the notebook she always kept in her bag. She fished it out ready to take with her to the phone box outside the post office. It was a nuisance not being able to get a signal on her mobile.

She got through to the office in town at once. 'Mr Woodley is away on holiday at the moment,' the receptionist told her in a sympathetic voice. 'Can it wait until he gets back next week or would you like his partner to deal with it?'

Cara hesitated. Although important to her, the matter might well be regarded as trivial. She imagined herself ushered into his office, the relevant file produced, paper extracted and studied. And then the partner pushing his glasses up from the end of his nose and regarding her kindly as he assured her that her grandfather's will had been proved, that there was nothing to worry about.

She took a deep breath, banishing the scene from her mind, and explained the position. The receptionist's voice dropped in pitch as she said she would make an appointment for Thursday, at three o'clock, for Cara to see Mr Hindstock and discuss the matter with him.

Cara replaced the receiver thoughtfully. She would put it out of her mind until then. She had plenty to do to keep her occupied, but first she needed to put more money on her mobile for when she had the chance to use it. She pushed open the post office door and went inside.

A few people were waiting at the grill. She saw that there were birthday cards, too, on the other side of a partition.

It would be a good idea to get a couple for friends' birthdays coming up in the next week or two. Pleased at being so well organised, Cara started to make her selection.

On the other side of the partition she heard Ellie Trevean's soft voice and Josh Pellew's deeper one. They seemed to be discussing something that made Josh's voice harsh and Ellie's placating.

'There might be a very good reason for it, love,' she heard Ellie say.

Josh gave a snort of annoyance. 'What good reason could there be for neglect, for not being there for him when he needed it?'

'But we don't know the whole story.'

'And don't need to. Selfish and uncaring, I'm afraid.'

There was the thump of something heavy being dropped and an exclamation from Ellie.

Cara thumbed through a few more cards and then put them back. Could they be discussing her or was she being paranoid?

She heard Josh's voice again, obviously addressing the postmaster, then the sound of footsteps and the door opening and closing.

As she came round the partition with two cards in her hand Ellie glanced at her in dismay. 'Oh m'dear, I didn't see you there.'

Cara smiled with an effort and waited her turn to be served. The flush on the other woman's face was almost the shade of her pink jersey and Cara felt dizzy for a moment from the red mist in front of her eyes.

She clenched her free hand. So Josh had been making wounding accusations about her, had he?

Poor Ellie hardly knew where to look at she folded the sheet of stamps she had purchased and put them in her bag. Cara paid for her cards and was ready to leave at the same time.

They walked together down the road. Cara couldn't speak at first for her anger at Josh's words.

Ellie cleared her throat. 'Are you

enjoying your holiday, m'dear?' she said hesitatingly.

'No holiday,' Cara said with difficulty. 'Not any more. This is my permanent home now.'

'Oh m'dear!'

'From this moment,' Cara said, sounding as firm as if she and Arlene had already reached an agreement on the matter.

Another crazy statement that seemed to sprout out of her mouth with no volition on her part. What was she thinking of? Oh well, she'd done it now.

She stopped dead. Best to burn her boats even more disastrously while she was about it so there was no going back.

'I've just remembered a couple more phone calls I've got to make,' she said.

Ellie said goodbye with a look of relief. And who could blame her, Cara thought. It was Josh who'd put her in this position, opening his big mouth and sounding off about something he knew nothing about.

She yanked open the door of the phone box and stepped inside, trying to calm down before she lifted the receiver. She breathed deeply and let her breaths out slowly. One, two, three, four, five. That was better.

As she had thought, the new owner of *Flower Power* made no objection about receiving her notice. 'Just put it in writing,' she said crisply. 'To take effect at the end of your leave.' Cara smiled. This was better than she had hoped.

Four weeks' notice was required to vacate her flat and that was all right too. She would need to return to it to clear out her belongings and bring them down here. She didn't dare think where she would put them in the event of the cottage having to go on the market. She would deal with that when the time came.

The last phone call to Arlene was the most difficult. How to explain what she had done in the light of Arlene's wish for her share of the selling price? She listened to her own voice making a mess of it.

'I'm coming down,' Arlene said when she paused to take a breath. 'Tom's mum can look after the kids for the weekend. I'll be down Friday, by train. Ring me Thursday night and I'll tell you the time of arrival. I'll need to be met.'

The furious tone in Arlene's voice seemed to linger in the air as Cara returned to the cottage. But what did she expect? Sweetness and light and, 'Of course you're doing the right thing!' Of course not, but she wasn't about to let Arlene's natural reaction spoil this moment of euphoria.

It lasted well into the morning. Cara tackled the cleaning of the bedroom with vigour, moving the heavy bed out from the wall as if it was no weight at all. By lunchtime she had the room looking as good as she could make it.

Arlene would sleep in here and wake to the view of the old sailing ship at her berth in the harbour and of the cottages and the hill behind. The sunshine would pour in, hiding the shabby carpet. She hoped.

Cara hummed to herself as she finished off upstairs. The sun was shining now. Outside called and what better way to spend the afternoon than starting a painting from up on the cliffs?

Quickly she packed up a couple of cheese sandwiches, filled a flask with coffee, grabbed an apple and filled her water jar. There was room for all this in the top of the canvas painting bag.

The tide was going out and the wet pebbles at the water's edge shone with a brilliance that was pleasing. She would forget the cliff top and work here instead. By the time she had set up her easel and attached a large canvas to it, the water had receded even further. Great.

She worked hard, totally absorbed. The painting went well. After a while she stood back to see the effect and was pleased with what she had done so far.

She had painted the harbour wall as a backdrop and got the myriad of subtle colours of the stone to perfection.

She didn't quite know how she had managed this, but was grateful for the inspiration the scene afforded her. The sea was more difficult and she bit her lip as she concentrated on the frilly wavelets flirting with the wet pebbles.

'Is it for sale?' asked a voice behind her.

Startled, she looked round and saw the smiling face of a man about her own age in navy shorts and T-shirt with an orange anorak slung over one arm. Over his other arm swung a video camera.

'Sorry to be peering over your shoulder,' he said deprecatingly as he moved back a step or two.

His grey eyes looked friendly. He tossed a lock of straight fair hair off his forehead.

'That's OK,' she said. 'Feel free.'

'So . . . d'you sell your work?' His voice had a pleasant tone to it and he sounded really interested.

'Are you a painter yourself?'

'A mere journalist from the local paper on duty this fine afternoon. My brother paints. He exhibits down in Falmouth.'

'Successfully?' Cara wiped her brush on a piece of kitchen towel, dipped it in her water jar and wiped it again.

'He doesn't do badly. He does abstracts. Some of them aren't bad. I haven't seen you round here before, have I?'

'Or me you,' she said, smiling.

'On holiday?'

'Not any more.' She picked up her palette knife and then put it down again. The mood had been broken. She had done enough for this afternoon. Glancing at her watch, she saw that it was much later than she had thought.

Her companion came forward again to examine her work more closely. 'You've caught the light on the water brilliantly.'

She smiled. Appreciation was always welcome and she could never get enough of it.

He lifted his head at the sound of an engine as a rubber dinghy appeared round the harbour wall, cruising slowly to shore. 'Hi there, Tristan,' a girl's voice called.

'Where's Josh? Isn't he with you?'

'Not coming till later,' came the reply. 'He'll meet us there.'

'See you around,' he called back to Cara as he ran to the water's edge, removing his trainers when he got there.

He was soon aboard and they were away. Cara began to pack away her painting gear. She lifted her painting, already dry, from the easel and laid it to one side so that she could fold the easel and fix the strap round it to keep it secure.

As she did so she heard the sound of scrunching pebbles and looked up to see Josh walking across the beach, looking as if he was brooding on some deep problem. His forehead creased into a frown as he saw who she was.

She pushed the kitchen roll into her

bag and picked up her easel.

He glanced at the painting and then away again, his face expressionless. 'Not working at the cottage then?'

'Not out with your friends?' she retorted.

He turned his back on her, looking out to sea. He was motionless long enough for her to pick up her painting and hold it protectively against her. Then he moved away, his long legs covering the expanse of pebbles to the path in seconds. There was no sign of him when she got there. Something had upset him, that was for sure.

How different he was this early evening from the friendly Tristan who had shown such interest in her work. She wondered where they were all going and if they would meet up as planned.

Up to now she hadn't felt lonely being here in Polmerrick on her own. Now, seeing the easy camaraderie between Tristan and the girl in the boat, it had brought home to her how it really was. So far she had concentrated only on the cottage and her grandparents, but now she knew there must be something else, too, if she was to feel at home here. Ellie Trevean was friendly, Eric Trubshaw too, but she needed people of her own age as well. Maybe when she found herself a job she would meet more people and get to know them.

Cara sighed as she walked up the road to the cottage, wondering for the first time if she was making a big mistake in wanting to settle here. But maybe she wouldn't be after all. When Arlene came raging down at the weekend demanding her share of the money from the property she might find that her days in Polmerrick were numbered.

On Friday evening Arlene's train was on time. Cara had only just managed to find a parking space in the station yard in St Austell and had got on to the platform when she saw her sister alighting from a carriage halfway along carrying a huge hold-all.

She rushed forward to greet her. 'What on earth have you got in there?' she asked breathlessly.

'Space,' said Arlene. 'If there's clearing out to be done I'll take some of my share of things back with me on Sunday.'

'There's not much of any use,' said Cara. 'Books, a photo album, one or two little knick-knacks, that's all. Though there's one thing that's really good, a book our grandfather wrote himself. I'm dying to show you.'

'Where's your car?' said Arlene, hoisting the straps of her bag over one shoulder.

Cara was glad that Arlene's first glimpse of Polmerrick and Bal Cottage was in daylight. The evening sun was just sliding behind the hill at the back of the cottage as they reached the village. The buildings on the other side of the harbour were bathed in the last rays.

Cara drove round to that side so that

they could look out across the narrow harbour to Bal Cottage, snug between its neighbouring buildings. It looked friendly and attractive, their own place. Mr Hindstock, the solicitor, had assured her of that when she went to see him, as she had known he would.

She opened her car door and out, going round to the other side of the car to open Arlene's door too. 'Come and see,' she said proudly.

5

'But it's so small,' Arlene objected, as she gazed at the little pink cottage with the thatched roof.

'That's because those buildings on either side are big.'

'Who owns those?'

Cara shrugged. 'They're warehouses of some sort, large storage sheds. One of them is full of planks of wood, I think. The other's empty at the moment. The cottage looks cosy, though, don't you think?'

'I suppose so.' Arlene was grudging.

'Come on, I'll take you back there. The beaches can wait till tomorrow, and the village.'

By the time Cara had parked the car and lugged Arlene's bag inside Bal Cottage the lights needed to be on. Arlene said nothing as Cara showed her the rooms downstairs and then went ahead of her up to the bedrooms. Arlene put down her holdall in the front one and looked out of the window. 'Not much of a view,' she complained.

Cara's spirits plummeted. First impressions were so important. When she had arrived that first day the sun gleamed on the pink walls of the front of the cottage and the thatch was steaming a little from the warmth of the sun. She wished it could have been like that for Arlene.

Maybe after a hot drink and some of the chicken casserole she had prepared earlier things would improve. But come to think of it no mouth-watering smells had greeted them when she unlocked the back door.

She rushed downstairs. The oven was cold. 'It'll have to be cheese on toast,' she said shamefacedly when Arlene joined her.

They ate it at the kitchen table. Then Arlene yawned and stretched. 'It's been a long day,' she said.

'You'll like it better in the morning,' said Cara, getting up to carry the plates to the sink. 'Go on up. I won't be long. We'll talk tomorrow.'

They hadn't spoken much as they drove out of town and took the road down to Polmerrick. Even Cara's enquiries about the children hadn't met with much response. It was obvious that something was worrying her sister.

The rain next day didn't help. Or the low cloud that hung over the hill on the other side of the harbour. It was too wet to show Arlene the pebble vortex on the bank and in the mood she was in she wouldn't have appreciated it anyway.

Cara pulled out the slim book their grandfather had written and carried it with the photo album through into the kitchen. Arlene thumbed through the pages as she finished eating her breakfast toast. Then she looked quickly at the photograph album, only pausing briefly to study the photo of the young couple on their wedding day.

'Our parents,' Cara told her. 'They

must be, don't you think?'

Arlene nodded as she snapped the book shut. 'So long ago,' she said sadly. 'And we never knew them. It's like looking at strangers. Minda looks a bit like her, though.'

'I thought that,' said Cara eagerly.

'But that doesn't alter anything.'

'Tell me what's wrong,' Cara said, placing her empty coffee mug on the table. 'Come on, Arlene, something's bothering you apart from the cottage. You might as well tell me what it is.'

Her sister hesitated, crumbling the last pieces on her plate. She looked pale this morning and there were dark shadows beneath her eyes. 'Nothing much. Not really. Only lack of cash, as always. Another bill came in yesterday morning and Tom was furious. But he likes me looking nice.'

Cara glanced at Arlene's soft green cashmere jersey that seemed to high-light the sheen in her brown hair.

Her own navy sweatshirt had dried mud on one cuff. She should have changed it. She pushed her long hair away from her face.

'We've got to talk about this place,' Arlene went on. 'No way can we keep it. Any rent you'd pay wouldn't be enough. I need a lump sum at once. Anyway it's a dump.'

'But I like it,' said Cara.

'We've got to get it on the market at once before it deteriorates any more. And what about the roof? When will that need to be done. We can't let it go through another winter.'

'The thatch is OK for a few more years,' said Cara defensively.

Arlene scraped her hair back and went to peer out of the small window over the sink. 'The rain's stopped,' she said. 'I'm going out. On my own. I need to get a feel of the place.'

Cara nodded. It might be best to let Arlene discover things for herself. She might find she liked Polmerrick. While she was gone she would tidy things up here and make the place look as presentable as she could. Maybe get some coffee going. Then they could discuss this properly.

Arlene came back glowing, a haze of moisture on her hair and a triumphant expression on her face.

'I've found out a few things,' she said, sitting down heavily on one of the rickety kitchen chairs. 'And arranged something too. We'll get out first estimate this afternoon.'

Cara was horrified. 'You haven't been to Pellew's?'

'We need more estimates of course.'

'Hey, wait a minute. I don't like the sound of this.'

'Mark Pellew was the chap I saw, big with a swarthy sort of face. Thinning hair. He'll come himself or send someone.'

'You're going too fast,' said Cara.

Arlene helped herself to a biscuit from the tin on the table. 'It can't be too fast if we want to get things moving.'

Cara poured water into two mugs she had ready and added milk. She pushed one across to Arlene and sat down herself. 'There must be a way round it,' she said. 'I see myself living in Polmerrick, making a career move. I want to paint, Arlene, and sell my paintings. And I want to live here.'

'You can paint anywhere.'

'It's my inspiration, this place. It seems to have got into my blood. I feel we have roots here in Polmerrick and that's important. Don't you want it too, the feeling that we belong somewhere because our grandparents home was here?'

'I'd rather have the money,' said Arlene.

Cara took a sip of coffee. 'I know it's asking a lot of you to agree to keep Bal Cottage,' she said slowly. 'Especially as you don't feel the same way about it as me.'

'You're frowning,' said Arlene.

'I haven't shown you the pebble vortex in the back garden,' said Cara. 'Made by our grandparents, Arlene. It's a link with them. When you see it you'll feel it too.'

Arlene laughed. 'Are you joking? We'll get our first estimate of the value this afternoon.'

A panicky feeling ran up Cara's spine. It was sounding too definite. 'Why don't we rent the cottage out as a holiday cottage?' she said breathlessly. 'There's definitely a market.'

Arlene's scornful glance around the kitchen told Cara what she thought of that suggestion. And Arlene was right. She hadn't stopped to think. A lot of money would be needed to do the place up to a required standard and how many weeks would that take even if they could arrange a loan? They couldn't expect an income from letting for a very long time. Too long for the state of Arlene's finances.

'Suppose I buy you out?' Cara said suddenly.

Arlene was astonished. 'You?'

Cara had surprised even herself. She didn't know where that idea had come from, but she liked it. All at once she felt confident and yet she had no good reason. She had a bit saved in the building society, but nowhere near enough. 'I'll get it somehow,' she said wildly. 'A bank loan . . . I'll get a job.'

Arlene laughed, not taking her seriously.

'I mean it, Arlene.'

'But you've got a job, in Exeter.'

'Not any more. Or a flat either, for much longer. I've given notice to leave both because I wanted to be in Polmerrick so much. Don't you see, it's a perfect idea. Oh Arlene, I should have thought of it at once.' Cara felt as if her face was on fire with her enthusiasm. She had no doubt it could work.

'But I need the money now.'

'A sale to anyone else will take a bit of time. A few weeks anyway. That'll give me time to get a loan organised, see the solicitor to get it all done properly.'

'You really mean it.'

Cara leapt up, unable to sit still. 'What time did you say this Mark Pellew's coming?'

Arlene tapped her fingers on the table in rhythmic dance. 'We'll need to get an average price . . . contact more estate agents and see what they say. This needs thinking about. You won't be able to get a loan if you haven't got a job already, will you?'

'I'll get one,' said Cara wildly. 'I'll start painting. I'll arrange for exhibitions to sell my work for hundreds of pounds.'

'You make it sound easy.'

'It is, oh it is.' Cara snatched up her mug and downed the rest of her coffee. If you wanted something badly enough you could make it happen. She'd read that somewhere once and now she would prove it to be true. She wanted Bal Cottage and nothing would stop her now. 'There's a job at the craft shop in the village advertised in their window. Did you see the notice? I'll go at once.' Cara felt carried along by her passion and wondered that Arlene still sat at the table looking bemused.

Her sister was still there when she got

back and slumped down in the chair opposite her. 'It's gone,' she said. She hadn't been able to believe it when she saw that the notice in the craft shop window had been taken down and she had gone inside to make sure.

'Only yesterday,' the woman said. 'I'm sorry, m'dear.' She had looked it too and Cara had almost burst into tears. Instead she had gone next door for a local paper. Now she spread it out on the table and opened it to the appointments page.

'I told you it wouldn't be easy,' Arlene said.

'You didn't,' Cara retorted, running her finger down the page.

'I thought you were going to show me round the place.'

'I thought you'd been on your own.'

'Not everywhere. Only to the shops and the estate agent.'

Cara looked up hopefully. 'I need a pen.' There was one in the pocket of her jacket and a small pad of paper. Hastily she jotted down a few numbers and picked up her mobile. 'Come on then. I might get a signal up on the cliffs.'

Arlene leaned across and reached for the paper. 'Oh well,' she said. 'It won't hurt to phone a couple more estate agents, will it?' She found what she wanted and Cara wrote down those numbers too. It felt as if she was getting somewhere.

The clouds were beginning to clear away now, the sky to the south showing a glimmer of light that caught the underside of them. There was a seat not far along the cliff path overlooking the larger of the two beaches. People were beginning to wander down to it and spreading themselves out for the day.

Sitting on either side of the seat, the girls set to work on their mobiles. Arlene finished first. 'That's done then,' she said with satisfaction, clicking off her mobile. 'One on Monday morning, one in the afternoon. You'll make sure you're in?'

'Of course,' said Cara absently. She wasn't having as much luck as she hoped. In fact none at all. 'Everywhere seems to be fixed up already,' she said. 'I can't believe it so early in the season. I don't really want a seasonal job though, do I? Permanent's what I'm after. But anything would do.' It wasn't going to be as easy as she thought but she wouldn't give up.

'There'll have to be a time limit,' said Arlene firmly. 'I can't hang about for ever.'

Cara nodded, running her finger down the page again in the hope she had missed something.

In fairness to Arlene she would have to agree to that. But hopefully it wouldn't come to that.

'So where's this other beach you told me about?' said Arlene. 'Then we'll have another walk up the road to the shops and grab something for lunch if there's somewhere handy.'

That Josh Pellew should be the one who came to measure up for the estimate shouldn't have surprised Cara in the least. In dismay she saw his dark head pass the kitchen window before he tapped on the back door. She gave a little gasp.

'I'll get it,' Arlene cried, rushing forward to open the door and greet him.

He came into the kitchen holding his clipboard, dressed this afternoon in dark trousers and a jacket with his blue shirt open at the neck. Cara had only seen him in casual clothes before. He nodded at Cara, but turned his attention to Arlene.

'I'm Josh Pellew from A. J. Pellew. You're Miss Karrivick?' he said, pronouncing the name in the way they did themselves.

'We both are,' said Arlene. 'I'm Arlene and this is Cara.'

He gave a slight ironic bow in Cara's direction. 'So where would you like me to start?'

'Here if you like,' said Arlene. 'Shall we keep out of your way?'

'As you wish,' he said He glanced at the tidy room, at the scrubbed table and then for a second at Cara. She saw that there was no sign of friendliness in his eyes, only a hint of scorn.

She had no intention of staying in the room anyway. Arlene would deal with things, talk to him when he had got all the measurements he needed. The last thing she wanted to witness was Arlene's enjoyment of it all even though Bal Cottage wasn't going on the open market.

She felt a little glow of satisfaction, but Josh didn't know that. She could hardly tell him now anyway. They had to discover the true value of the property and this was the only way of going about it.

At first she had felt awkward about it. Arlene had no such qualms. Although she hung back she obviously wanted to be involved and was already offering to hold one end of the tape for him.

Cara left them to it and slipped out into the garden, glad of the fresh air on her face. She squatted on part of the retaining wall and studied the piece of vortex pattern of pebbles on the bank that she had uncovered so far. What would her grandparents do if they had her sort of problem, she wondered? Someone . . . her grandmother? . . . had spent hours on this.

She must have cared about it a lot. It would have given her happiness and peace of mind. Cara sighed, understanding how it would have been because of the satisfaction she got from her painting. She knew that living here was the way forward for herself. She wouldn't give up.

After a while Cara went back inside and heard voices from upstairs and then the clatter of footsteps as Josh and Arlene came down again and into the kitchen. Josh stood leaning on the door jamb busily writing, the lines deepening on his forehead.

'Had you a price in mind Miss . . . er . . . Karrivick?'

Arlene glanced at Cara who said nothing. She felt Josh's eyes on her for a moment but wouldn't look at him.

'We need your estimate, Mr Pellew,' said Arlene. 'We need to know what the place is worth.'

Josh clicked shut his Biro. 'Thank you for thinking of us. Hopefully we'll be able to act for you. You'll be getting a couple of front door keys cut, of course.'

'And the estimate?' asked Arlene eagerly.

He glanced at Cara. 'Our estimate will be with you in a few days.'

Arlene was crestfallen. 'I hoped you could give it now.'

'No can do. It needs thinking about.'

'Thank you,' Cara said firmly. She moved to one side to let him pass, but he stopped beside her.

'I'm surprised,' he said quietly before making for the door.

'So what's going on?' Arlene demanded when he had gone.

Cara shrugged. 'Nothing as far as I know.'

'Don't tell me that. The man can't keep his eyes off you.'

'I didn't notice,' said Cara. She hadn't wanted to notice. Josh was nothing to her. 'I'm going out for a bit, down to the small beach this side? Coming?'

'Not me,' said Arlene. 'I'll have a rout around in the junk room and see what I can find.'

To Cara's dismay she saw Josh seated in a car parked a short way down the road. He had removed his jacket and slung it on the back seat. He seemed to be looking at the old sailing ship, but as he became aware of her approach he turned and wound down his window. 'I'd like a word,' he said.

She looked at him in silence.

'We need to talk,' he said, opening his door and springing out.

Cara moved back. 'I don't think so. There's nothing to say.'

'Come on, get in,' he said with authority. 'There are a few things I need to know about this business.'

6

Cara stared at Josh in amazement. 'On whose behalf?' she asked, staring into his eyes.

He met her gaze with a purposeful one of his own. 'My own, I think. I need to know something and you're the person to tell me.'

She was taken aback at his nerve. No way she was going to jump into his car and be whisked off for a heart-to-heart with Josh Pellew. True, Arlene had asked his family firm to give them an estimate of a suitable selling price, but that committed them to nothing. And it certainly didn't give him the right to interrogate her about their plans now when he had criticised her so forcibly to Ellie Trevean as selfish and uncaring.

'I don't think so,' she said quietly. 'I have nothing to say to you, here or anywhere else.'

He took a step forward. 'We could talk more comfortably in The Miners' Rest, that's all. Won't you come?'

'I think you've said enough already,' she said, retreating a little. 'You're entitled to your own opinions, but not to spread them around where they can hurt people. Especially if they're not true. It's simply not fair.'

'What are you talking about?' He looked so bewildered that for a moment she wondered if she had dreamt his comments to Ellie that she had overheard, or that he was referring to someone else.

She stared back at him. 'I think you know.' Was that the dawning of comprehension she saw in his eyes? 'So no thanks to the Miners' Rest or anywhere else,' she added.

He frowned. 'I'm concerned about certain things in the cottage, that's all. I feel that there are things your grandfather valued that haven't yet come to light.'

She looked at him suspiciously. 'And

what might they be?'

'That's just it. I don't know. We need to talk about it.'

'But are they any concern of yours?'

'I was fond of him. I understood him. I just want to know.'

'Is that why you came to measure up the cottage so you could have a good nose round?'

'No, of course not. In any case your sister was watching me like a hawk.' A brief smile touched his lips and was gone again.

'I assure you that you have no legal claim to the cottage,' Cara said sharply, starting to move away. 'There's nothing we can do about it even if we wanted to.'

'Wait! I haven't finished.'

'You have as far as I'm concerned.'

She had intended to walk down to the beach and he wasn't going to stop her. As she set off she heard him slam the car door, but there was no sound of the engine.

She quickened her pace, determined

to ignore him. It was ridiculous to fear being chased down the main street, but she wasn't about to be bullied into doing something she didn't want to do.

By the time she reached the slipway to the beach she heard him right behind her. She swung round as she got to the pebbles. 'Leave me alone.'

He was breathing heavily, his eyes gleaming. For a moment she thought he would grab her and lunged away so quickly she lost her balance. He leapt forward to catch her and she felt his rapid heart beat through his shirt as he saved her from the threatened fall. His grip on her arms was strong, but she struggled free, gasping. 'I've got nothing to tell you.'

He let her go gently. 'Let me be the judge of that, Cara, please. Let's sit on this rock for a minute.'

She tried to refuse, but something made her do as he said. Maybe it was his use of her name for the first time that weakened her resolve. For the moment she was glad to sit next to him and lean back against the wall to listen to what he had to say.

This wasn't much, because he didn't know what might have been in the cottage before Jack Karrivick died that was important to the old man. It was just this feeling he had, he told her, that there might be something else.

'I've searched through everything,' she told him simply. She glanced at Josh sideways. It occurred to her that he might have wondered if there had been a later will. If so she hadn't found one. 'I wouldn't destroy anything important,' she added.

He nodded as if he believed her.

'I'd like to know more about my grandfather,' she said and then wished she hadn't because he thought she should have known these things for herself and had chosen not to. She clenched her hands together, hurt that he should think that of her and not wanting to state her own case because of it.

'What do you want to know?'

'I talked to the curator at the museum. He told me about the book of shipwrecks.'

'Wreckers,' said Josh.

'Yes, that. And of how my grandfather worked with him for some time.'

He nodded, but said nothing for a moment as he gazed down at the line of brown seaweed the falling tide had left behind. She noticed that the rubber dinghy he often kept here wasn't in its usual place by the harbour wall. Perhaps Tristan had been using it again, he and the girl she had seen with him the other day.

There was a sudden shout. Josh leapt to his feet. 'I must go,' he said.

Cara nodded, but he didn't see because he was off without a backward glance. The spell in which she had found herself was broken and that was no bad thing. It was a moment of madness sitting here with Josh who had made no secret of his opinion of her. What had she been thinking of?

She got up and walked across to the

other side of the beach to where the dark cliffs towered. She had problems enough without dealing with Josh Pellew's concerns about her grandfather's belongings, lost or otherwise.

She had to work out the best way to raise the sum of money needed for Arlene's share of the cottage. She must concentrate all her thoughts on that. Her sister wouldn't wait forever. Couldn't wait if what she said about her pressing debts was true.

* * *

Arlene went off on the train on Sunday evening looking more cheerful than when she had arrived. 'Don't forget to get moving on raising the money,' were her last words. 'Four weeks you've got, Cara. All right?'

Very much all right, Cara thought as she drove herself back to Polmerrick. It was good to have that time especially as Pellew's had a prospective buyer already. If what Josh had said was true, of course. Four weeks seemed ample time to get things moving her end.

She still had two weeks of her paid holiday left and could devote tomorrow at least to getting started on another painting. Then she would get down to some serious job-hunting. Soon the estimates would be in and she and Arlene could agree on a fair price.

She was up early next morning and was up on the cliff path as soon as her bank in town opened to phone for an appointment about a loan. She arranged a suitable time for the following day. She had to stay in today for the arrival of the next estate agent to measure up and again this afternoon for the third one.

The sunshine felt warm on her face as Cara set up her easel in front of the cottage. By the time the estate agent arrived she had made a charcoal sketch of the old sailing vessel with the cottages on the hill on the other side of the harbour as a backdrop. She had also painted in the sky and begun on the ship itself before the shadows changed.

She hummed to herself as she worked, liking the faint salty breeze on her face and pleased that she was making a good start and that the sunshine highlighted the subject she had chosen in a way that was specially appealing.

The estate agent, a woman this time in smart navy suit and yellow blouse, made short work of measuring the rooms with Cara's help, but made much point of examining the outside of the property with narrowed eyes. When she had gone Cara set to work again, anxious now to complete her painting in one day if all went well.

She needed to build up a portfolio, to have plenty to show if she was lucky enough to find somewhere to exhibit them. She might even have time to complete from memory the painting of the beach she had begun the other evening.

The afternoon estate agent came early and after he had gone Cara returned to her easel to view her work as critically as she could. Then she picked up her brush and was so totally absorbed in her work that the hours flew. At last she put in the finishing touch, dipped her brush in her water jar and wiped it on a piece of handy paper towel.

'Can we have a look then?' someone asked.

She looked up, startled, to see a family group eyeing her with interest.

She put her brush down and turned the easel to face them. A bit of feedback was welcome.

'Is it for sale?' the mother asked.

'Oh yes,' Cara said. 'All my work's for sale. I plan to have a mini-exhibition here on Saturday if you're interested.' Again she had come out with something that had surprised herself. It was getting to be a habit. But why not? This wide area of paving was ideal, especially as the cottage was on the way to the beaches with plenty of people passing by. She'd have to work fast, though, to have enough ready by then.

The family made murmurings of interest and moved on. Cara replaced today's painting on the easel with her unfinished beach scene and put a few swift touches to that.

Then she began to pack up, tired after the day's work, but glowing inside with the encouragement she was feeling. About to carry everything to the back of the cottage, she turned and saw Tristan Perry walking down the road in light trousers and jacket.

He waved. 'Been busy?' He whistled as he saw the finished beach scene. 'Wow, some painting!'

'I'm thinking of doing more local scenes for sale and displaying them out here. What do you think?'

'Brilliant,' he said, moving his briefcase from one hand to the other. 'You'll be a sensation.'

'I've done two so far,' she said. 'Luckily acrylic dries fast. I must find a framer tomorrow in town. I'm aiming for my first display on Saturday.'

'You'll do it, easy,' he said, smiling his encouragement. 'Like me to do a write-up about it for my paper? Local interest, you see. An instant interview with you now. How about that?'

She laughed as he opened his briefcase and extracted pad and pen. There wasn't much to tell him, but he seemed satisfied.

'I hope so. I'm job-hunting too,' she said when he had finished.

He raised his eyebrows. 'There's a job going up the road if you're interested. Not exactly intellectually demanding but it's reasonable money.'

'How do you know?'

He grinned. 'Inside information. I worked there myself once, but not scrubbing floors.'

Light dawned. 'A cleaning job,' she said. 'At Pellew's? No thanks.'

'Cleaning's beneath you?'

'It's not that.'

'The workforce?'

She shrugged. 'I suppose I'd be working after the office was closed every day? I'll be working on my own?'

'Got it in one,' he said. 'And Ellie Trevean won't eat you.'

Cara thought about it. 'The hours would be perfect,' she said. 'I'd have time to paint during the day or even to get another job too. And I like Ellie.'

'Who doesn't? She's a great friend of mine,' Tristan said warmly. 'Kind to me when I worked there. She'll see you right.'

'I haven't got the job yet,' said Cara, smiling.

'Get yourself there first thing tomorrow,' Tristan advised. 'You'll walk it, believe me.'

And of course the hours of work for anyone wanting to do other things as well couldn't be better. Ellie was the one with the power to appoint the office cleaner and she was only too delighted to offer the job to Cara.

'I've been doing as much as I can myself,' she confided, unbuttoning the top buttons on her fluffy mauve cardigan. 'I'm so pleased you want it, m'dear.' She fanned her hand back-wards and forwards in front of her flushed face.

They arranged that Cara should start that evening, arriving half-an-hour before the office closed as Ellie could show Cara where everything was and tell her what was expected of her.

Happy that things were beginning to work out well, she went back to the cottage to make herself presentable for the trip to town.

The estimate from A. J. Pellew was on the front doormat when Cara got back and she picked it up and carried it through to the kitchen. It was lower than she had thought it would be. Was this because the firm was hoping for a quick sale with the client that Josh told them about? Himself?

Suspicion gnawed at her as she put the paper back in the envelope and wedged it for safe keeping beneath the coffee jar on the table. A good thing the estimate was only one of three. In any case she must wait until she had received the others before contacting her sister.

The bank manager had refused a loan.

She still couldn't believe it. There were other banks, though. She must get on to them tomorrow. But if one bank refused her wouldn't the others too? She knew they would, but refused to consider that for the moment. This afternoon she would paint and think of nothing else until it was time to go to Pellew's.

'There, m'dear,' said Ellie Trevean with satisfaction. 'Anyone can see you know what you're doing. A lucky day for us when you came along.'

Cara smiled. 'I don't know about that.' Ellie had tidied everything up so well that the main office was easy to clean. There were other rooms too, of course, darker and more cluttered, but they would be no problem. One door was closed.

'Always kept locked,' Ellie told her as she got the vacuum cleaner out of the cupboard. 'Only Josh has the key of that, m'dear, and he looks after it himself. It's the headquarters of his survey team.'

'Sounds important.'

'They think so. Threw himself into it, he did, when that girl, Maggie, let him down last year. Four weeks before the wedding, if you please. Said he'd never trust any woman again and I'm feared he means it. A bad time, that. I was heart-sorry, but no-one could do anything.' Ellie looked troubled. She pushed the cupboard door shut with one shoulder. 'Bring it all through into the office, m'dear,' she said.

Cara did as she said and began to assemble the vacuum cleaner, trying not to imagine the hurt Josh must have felt.

Ellie sighed. 'He locked himself in his room for days on end. Said he was setting up some database or other. Now all he thinks about is finding bits of old wood along the beaches with those other two. Black he says they have to be, with traces of fastenings gone green or such like with bits of shells or pebbles stuck to them. Shows they've been submerged a long time you see. Polmerrick Maritime Survey Branch they call themselves. Something like that, anyway. I don't know the half of it.'

Cara slotted the brush on to the end and was ready for action. She had already dusted the main room.

'I'll leave you to it then, m'dear. You've got your key to lock up?'

Cara patted the pocket of her jeans and Ellie left, first opening a drawer in the desk and extracting a voluminous blue bag made of some soft material.

Cara worked hard when she had gone, making quite sure that everything was replaced exactly as she found it. Then she locked the door behind her and returned to Bal Cottage.

Since she had hardly eaten anything all day she made scrambled eggs that she ate with tomatoes and toast at the kitchen table. Then she found a banana and made coffee, carrying it out on a tray into the garden.

So Josh was gathering information about shipwrecks so far uncovered? She had noticed a boatload of divers when she was on the cliffs and had wondered what they were looking for. Maybe they were identifying remains of wrecks that lay forgotten off the coast. Her grandfather's book had told the story of many wrecks and some of those might still be down there somewhere. Fascinating to think of what might lie beneath the surface of the sea.

She yawned and stretched. It had been a long day. Tomorrow must be even longer. She had more canvasses and boards to prepare and must be up early to do it.

The two remaining estimates were much higher than the one from Pellew's. Thoughtfully Cara worked out the average before phoning Arlene. The price they agreed on was fair, Cara thought, but far more than she could possibly raise unless she could get a loan.

Her savings amounted to less than five per cent needed. As soon as a contract was drawn up between them for the sale to her of Arlene's half of the cottage she would hand this over as the deposit.

Even though she suspected that they wouldn't view her application with any favour the first thing to do, of course, was to visit the other banks in town. She had to try everything. Meanwhile she would work hard at her painting ready for Saturday.

7

Cara pulled the curtains open on Saturday morning with a feeling of relief. Blue sky and not a cloud, great! Just what she wanted to be able to set up early.

After a quick breakfast she unearthed some packing cases from the storeroom and placed them outside against the cottage wall to display some of the framed paintings. Her easel housed another, one of Bal cottage from the other side of the harbour that she particularly liked. She placed several unframed canvases flat on the ground. It all looked good to her so far.

She seated herself on a stool with a board on her lap and her wet water palette and water jar at her side and set to work on another painting. People liked to see her engrossed in producing her scenes and were happy to stand watching as she applied each brush-stroke.

She worked steadily. Today the shadows flickered a little in the breeze and made interesting patterns on the low wall opposite. Her first sale came from a young couple who stood admiring a painting of the clifftop for some time before making the decision to buy.

It was a good start. When Tristan appeared a little later she was able to tell him that things were beginning to move. He seated himself on one of the two stools she had brought outside and offered encouragement with such charm she felt a glow of optimism that everything was going to be all right.

Smiling, she accepted all he said, glad that she had taken the trouble to put on her new white shirt with the pink embroidery, the same shade as the shorts she was wearing for the first time.

'I like your painting of this fine cottage,' Tristan said. He got up to examine it closely, his face almost touching the canvas. 'A masterpiece. You've got yourself another sale. My sister will love it. I expect you've seen Gina around the place. She seems to know you.'

'The girl with you in the boat the other evening?'

'That's the one. It's her birthday on Tuesday.'

Several passers-by stopped to look. One of them seemed interested in the cottage painting too and Tristan breathed an exaggerated sigh of relief when they moved on without buying it.

'If you're serious you'd better take it off the easel now,' Cara said, smiling, as she leaned forward to dip her brush in the water.

Tristan smiled too. 'I might even do that.' He leaned back and put his hands behind his fair head. 'On the other hand I might leave it where it is for some other lucky person to buy. You'd paint me another just like it wouldn't you, Cara dear?'

She laughed as she unscrewed her tube of cerulean blue acrylic and added another dollop to her palette. 'Who knows?'

In the event, no-one bought the painting Tristan wanted, but four of the other framed ones and three unframed were sold by lunchtime. Afterwards everything slowed down for a while, but just as she was starting on the packing away an elderly couple approached and bought three.

Flushed with the success of the day, Cara wrapped up the painting of the cottage for Tristan, allowing him a generous discount. 'For your help and encouragement,' she told him.

'In that case watch out,' he said, his eyes twinkling. 'I'll be chivvying you up for more exhibitions every day,' he said, taking it from her. 'And look who's coming now. Another customer?'

But Josh wasn't that and she could see from the frowning expression on his face that he didn't approve of what he was seeing. He stood for a moment examining the few paintings stacked on the packing cases against the wall. Then his gaze flicked to Tristan. 'You do know about the Polmerrick byelaws, don't you?' he said sharply.

Tristan shrugged. 'Cool it, Josh. No need to be a spoilsport.'

'No buying and selling on pavements or forecourts. I'm surprised she hasn't been apprehended.'

Tristan gave a snort of a laugh. 'You can't be serious. A posse of policemen brandishing handcuffs and carting off our Cara?'

Cara giggled at the thought.

'As serious as I'll ever be,' said Josh, looking grim. 'There could be trouble. Don't say I didn't warn you.'

Serious now, Cara looked from one to the other. 'You mean I'm not allowed to sell my paintings outside my own property?'

'Exactly that. Be careful, that's all.'

He strode off.

'Wow!' Tristan laughed again, but this time he didn't sound as confident as before. 'That's Josh Pellew for you. I don't know what my sister sees in him.'

'But he's speaking the truth?'

'Well yes, if you want to be pedantic.'

'I want everything to be above board.' Cara frowned. This was a setback if it was true. The day had gone so well that already she was planning others. With hard work during each week she could do this every Saturday. Josh had been wrong about the cottage, hadn't he?

Suppose he was just trying it on now, not wanting her to raise enough cash to buy Arlene's share? This would need thinking about.

It wasn't until she had set up her easel on the cliff top next day that Cara remembered that Josh knew nothing about her arrangement with Arlene. She had discussed it with no-one and certainly not with Josh or with Ellie who might have passed on the information.

She knew Josh owned a house set back a little from the village because

Ellie had told her so what did he want with her cottage? But she wouldn't think about that now in the flush of composing another painting.

She was doing something positive about raising money, however little compared with the amount she needed. Until the banks opened tomorrow she could do nothing about trying to get a loan elsewhere. And at least she'd have some money to pay in.

There were several aspects from up here that would make good compositions and she made several before deciding on the one to do first. As usual she soon became engrossed. The sound of voices disturbed her at last and she looked up to see the elderly couple who had liked her work yesterday.

'Busy, I see,' said the woman pleasantly.

'We're interested in your work,' the man said. 'Martin's the name, Robert and Audrey.' He pulled out a card and handed it to her. 'We live on the edge of Bodmin Moor. Give us a ring some time. I wonder … do you take commissions?'

Cara flushed with pleasure. 'Of course.' She would gladly paint anything a customer wanted even though she found working that way worrying in case the proposed purchaser was disappointed in what she produced.

He looked pleased. 'Then could we come and see you again? When you've built up another body of work perhaps?'

'Of course,' said Cara again. This was better than taking commissions and she would be pleased to see them anyway. If only she had a larger space for displaying her work now that the forecourt of the cottage was out of bounds.

On the way home she noticed the empty storage shed near Bal Cottage. Cleared out it would be ideal. Why hadn't she thought of it before? Fired with enthusiasm, she planned how she would arrive at work early tomorrow so that she could talk to Ellie about it before she left.

Next day Cara did a good day's work. In the afternoon she drove into town to leave three more acrylic paintings to be framed and to make more enquiries about loans, all futile. No surprise there, but she was disappointed. Suppose she hadn't got anywhere after the six weeks she and Arlene had agreed before putting the cottage on the market?

At best, after that, she'd only be able to live here for a few months while the sale went through. During that time she would have to sort out somewhere to live and that might not be easy if she wanted to stay in Polmerrick.

Cara carried a mug of coffee out into the back garden when she got back. She deserved a rest, a chance to unwind a little before making a start on another painting before it was time to start her evening job. She wasn't hungry but she took some bread and cheese out too.

Eating slowly, she contemplated the

part of the pebble vortex she had uncovered so far. Such a lovely pattern of pebbles to go round and round for ever. One day she'd bring more back from the beach to complete the work, hopefully when the cottage was hers.

'That old place belongs to Mark Pellew,' Ellie told her as she bent to lock one of the drawers in her desk. 'He lets it out to firms needing to store things. Someone's taken it for six months.'

'They have?' Cara said in disappointment. 'It would have been great for somewhere to hold exhibitions of my work.'

'There's an old sail loft above,' said Ellie thoughtfully. 'Have you seen the stone staircase up to it round the side? He owns that too.'

'Is that in use?'

Ellie shook her head, and then patted a stray lock of brown hair into place. 'Not at the minute. Are you interested?'

'Oh Ellie, yes.'

Ellie smiled. 'I hear you're doing well

with your paintings. Mark'll be in the office first thing tomorrow. Do you want me to have a word?'

'Please,' said Cara, preparing to start on the cleaning of the inner rooms. She had worked out a system and wanted to get started. As she worked she could see herself ensconced in the sail loft, a good name for a gallery.

The Sail Loft had a good nautical ring for a gallery near the sea. She smiled as she imagined her masterpieces hung on cream-washed walls with crowds of interested people wandering about and buying. So real was it that it lingered in her mind until next day when she knew Ellie had had time to talk to Mark Pellew. She could wait no longer.

She could tell at once from Ellie's expression that it hadn't gone well.

'I'm sorry, m'dear.' Ellie looked crestfallen. She picked up a piece of paper and then put it down again. 'I did try. The best he could offer was a high rent, too high for that place. Rat-infested, I shouldn't wonder. And cold in winter.' She named a price that made Cara gasp.

'But why?' she said. 'It's empty, isn't it? Who else would want it?' She thought suddenly of Josh. Had he anything to do with the high rent demanded for the old sail loft? It seemed more than likely now she had time to think of it. Obviously he wanted her out of Bal Cottage for whatever reason and he might think that this was one way of encouraging her to give up on it.

She sat up straight. No way was she going to give in so easily. She would fight to stay, to make a new life here where she felt she belonged, to learn to know her grandparents through the lives they led here, to understand their hopes and interests.

'He didn't tell me why he won't let you have it at a reasonable rent say, but he was adamant,' said Ellie sadly.

This was a blow when her hopes had been raised, but it wasn't Ellie's fault. Cara turned away, trying not to show

how much she minded.

'I had a word at the shop,' Ellie went on.

'The shop?'

'Call in there, why don't you? Bob Cluny said he'd put a couple of your paintings in the window for you. Not much, I'm afraid, but better than nothing.'

'Oh Ellie, that's great,' Cara said. 'I'll go straight away. Thanks Ellie. You're a real pal.'

Ellie beamed as Cara went out and shut the door behind her.

Later Cara walked up the road past the shop for the pleasure of seeing two views of the beach displayed prominently in the shop window. She wondered how Gina, Tristan's sister, had liked her birthday present. Would she have preferred a general view of the village rather than one of Bal Cottage?

Now she came to think of it, this was a strange choice. Ah well, Tristan knew his sister best. He hadn't understood what Gina saw in Josh either.

Cara shied away from that thought, painful in spite of her efforts to put Josh from her mind. She went past the shop window twice, glad that it was after closing time so that no-one saw her interest in it. To her dismay she saw Tristan walking jauntily towards her.

He grinned when she came close. 'Just the person I wanted to see. I've got tickets for my brother's preview evening at his gallery in Falmouth tomorrow. Fancy coming? Six o'clock to eight. Champagne and eats, you can't miss it.'

'I can,' she said regretfully. 'I'm a working girl now. My hours won't let me.'

His disappointment was obviously real. 'What time do you finish tonight?'

'Eight,' she said.

'Then come out for a drink with me then.'

'But I can't stay long. I've work to do.'

'All work and no plays makes Jill a dull girl,' Tristan said, laughing at her.

'Come on, my love, relax a little. I won't keep you late. Promise and hope to die!'

She laughed and looked down at her old T-shirt and jeans. 'Like this? I'll need ten minutes to change.'

'You're on,' he said with satisfaction.

They went to the Miners' Rest and sat at a table outside overlooking the narrow harbour. Two motor cruisers were berthed there now as well as the old vessel and it was interesting to look down on them and watch the crews as they relaxed on board.

Cara was glad Tristan hadn't wanted to go somewhere else. Time was precious and when she got back she wanted to cut some mounts for the paintings she would sell unframed . . . or hoped to sell, she amended her thoughts swiftly.

'Did your sister like her present?' she asked as she sipped her elderflower cordial.

Tristan took a long drink from his pint glass. 'I haven't given it to her yet.

She's gone off somewhere this evening on a long-standing date with Josh Pellew. I tell her not to trust him an inch, but she won't listen.'

Cara felt an instant stab of pain she tried hard to suppress. 'I see.'

The girl in the boat with the two men must have been Gina, Tristan's sister. Ellie had said Josh would never trust a girl again after his broken engagement last year, but she was obviously wrong. But this was nothing to her so why did she feel as if she had had a sharp blow? She moved slightly in her chair as if by doing so she could be free of the feeling that something was missing from her life.

'What's up?' Tristan asked, rocking back on his chair so that the two rear feet of it sank into the grass.

Cara did her best to smile, but was afraid he would see the effort it took. 'What should be wrong?'

'Any luck with finding suitable premises for your gallery?'

She shook her head. 'I made

enquiries about the old sail loft near Bal Cottage, but the rent's too high for me. I'd be making a loss if I took it.'

'How about outlets in the towns? Art shops, I mean, craft shops too. They might display some of your work.'

'Worth a try,' Cara agreed. 'But I'll have to replenish my stock first.'

'And when you have I'll come with you. I know the area and can point out any places you might miss. I often have an assignment locally. It could all fit in.'

'Thanks.' Cara looked at him gratefully as he sat opposite her, totally relaxed. His company was soothing and she needed that at the moment. She needed his encouragement too and his friendship.

When at last they got up to go the evening shadows were lengthening and there was a coolness in the air that made her shiver. He pulled her close as they reached Bal Cottage and his kiss was long and breathtaking.

For a moment she relaxed against him. Then she pulled away, gasping. He made no attempt to detain her further and for that she was grateful.

'Another time,' he murmured as they parted.

The memory of his kiss was with her as she worked on the mounts. When at last she finished and was preparing for the night she lingered at her open bedroom window, gazing out at the old ship at her berth opposite with a surprising feeling of contentment.

8

Cara stared at Pellew's window in disbelief. There, right in the centre, was her painting of Bal Cottage. Beneath it, in bright blue lettering, was an advertisement for holiday cottages. The implication was obvious . . . this place is on the market for letting. How long had it been here displaying her home to the world's gaze? At least all day. And who had done this callous thing?

Heat flooded her face and for a moment she was unable to move. Then a little sobbing breath escaped her. Tristan? His sister? Josh? It could be any of them. But why, why? As a practical joke? She felt for the key with trembling fingers and unlocked the door.

Inside, she flopped down in Ellie's chair and stared at the back of the offending painting. It was humiliating to think that someone would do this thing knowing it would upset her. She wanted to close her eyes, to sleep and then waken to find it all a dream.

But it wasn't a dream and somehow she had to cope with it. Simple to remove the painting from the window and take it home with her. Physical reactions could be simple, but not the mental feeling of betrayal that left her feeling weak.

She sprang up and ran to the cupboard where the vacuum cleaner was kept. Feverishly she began to clean, rushing from one job to another until she was exhausted. The office had never looked so clean, so sterile. When she had finished and everything put away she found the key to the window display in the tray on Ellie's desk. With set face she unlocked it and removed the painting, then locked up again and replaced the key.

With the front of the painting held towards her she locked the front door of the premises, walked briskly to Bal

Cottage, thrust the painting into the stockroom room and slammed the door. Leaning against it, she took several deep breaths, still dazed by seeing her work in Pellew's window and not knowing how it had got there.

Who had wanted the painting on display in the one place that would most hurt her? Surely not Tristan, so pleased with it as a present for his sister? Or Gina either. How likely was she to agree to it being taken from her as soon as she had received it?

So . . . Josh? Had he persuaded Gina to lend it to him and she, not knowing exactly why, had agreed to please him? That idea hurt Cara but it seemed most likely.

She would do nothing more than she had already. Tomorrow, early, she would take herself and her painting gear off somewhere where no-one would find her and remain there until it was time to work at Pellew's when the office was closed for the day.

Let them wonder, whoever had done

it. She wouldn't be around to answer questions or to tell them what she had done with the painting. They wouldn't get it back until she decided to relinquish it.

Next morning she was glad that the sky was overcast and the trees on the hill at the back of the cottage were bending in the rising wind. The conditions suited her mood as she set off up the cliff path to the west. She knew she would come to more bays, more beaches and there she would work until she tired. She had brought three prepared boards with her.

The wind ruffled her hair as she found a suitable location on a beach that could only be reached down a precariously narrow path. This suited her needs well.

She slithered down the last part and landed on the soft golden sand, her canvas bag coming undone in the process. She laughed as she gathered up the tubes of paint and the brushes and palette knife that had fallen out and brushed her straying hair out of her eyes.

In some measure she forgot the events of the day before because as always she became totally engrossed when she was working. She was pleased with the composition of rocks, cliffs and sea and found she was enjoying plastering on thick acrylic colours of blues and greens. This one would be executed with the palette knife only. Already the textures were satisfying and it was as unlike the smoothness and detail of her painting of the cottage as she could manage.

She had brought food and drink and paused for lunch when the painting was nearly complete. Sometimes they worked to her satisfaction immediately. At others this was far from the case and she needed to return to work on them day after day. But not here in this wild and beautiful place.

The tide was going out and glistening sand greeted the emerging sunshine as the clouds rolled away. She felt a tingling in her fingertips. This was the way she liked it, the urge to work and work fast.

Later she decided to move on, to discover more locations to possibly use another day. The next beach, round a wooded headland, was accessible by road.

She saw people on the beach, a kiosk selling ice-cream, the masts of sailing dinghies up above and two people bringing a rattling boat on its trolley down the steep slipway to the beach. Plenty here to occupy her. She would make quick charcoal sketches of all that was going on and work on them later at Bal Cottage.

Her mobile rang. Cara jumped and pulled it out of her bag.

'Please, Cara, you've got to help me,' Arlene said urgently as soon as Cara clicked it on. 'I need money, now.'

Cara held it away from her ear, glad that her sister had caught her on the way home rather than at Bal Cottage where she had no signal. 'But why,

Arlene? What for?'

'Oh, Cara, please. You're my only hope.'

'But what's happened?'

'It's bad, really bad.' The desperation in Arlene's voice told her how serious this was.

'But Tom . . . '

Arlene sounded near to tears. 'Tom will kill me.'

'You haven't told him?'

'I can't, I can't. Not yet.'

This was terrible. 'Arlene, you must tell me. I'll help you, but you'll have to tell me what it's all about.'

'I . . . can't. You'll hate me too.'

'As bad as that?'

'And worse.' Arlene broke off, sobbing.

It was clear that she was unable to say more now. Cara bit her lip, considering. 'It's too late to do anything now,' she said. 'I can't get to town before the bank closes. It'll have to be tomorrow. I'll take my savings out . . . '

'But it won't be enough,' Arlene wailed.

'Listen Arlene. I'll do the best I can, I

promise, but I've got to think and you've got to tell me what all this is about. I'll phone again from work . . . no, you phone me, in about an hour. I'll have had time to work something out.'

As she gave the number she thought how hopeless it was. It sounded as if Arlene was in some deep trouble, worse even than being in debt. She could drive up to Exeter after work tonight if need be.

Cara returned to Polmerrick the way she had come, making a huge effort not to think of the only way for Arlene to obtain the large amount of money she implied she needed. It was a nightmare and she couldn't dwell on it until she had spoken to Arlene again when she was calmer.

As she passed she glanced down at the beach she had discovered earlier. The tide was well out now, licking some pieces of black wood. On impulse she left her gear at the top and went down the path to investigate. She tried to move a piece with the toe of her trainer, but it wouldn't budge. She saw that a mass of shells clung to it as if it had been their home for a long time.

She moved back from it and stood looking down. Waterlogged black wood with shells clinging to it meant that it had been in the water a long time.

From her visit to the museum in Polmerrick she knew that it could quite likely mean that a shipwreck had recently been exposed by sediment movement and was beginning to break up.

It should be reported straight away and the museum was the obvious place to find out how to go about it. And from Josh, of course, but she shied away from that idea. In any case she couldn't think straight at the moment in spite of her efforts.

Cara knew, by the time she got to work that there was little she could do to help Arlene financially unless she agreed to sell Bal Cottage. The knowledge was heavy on her heart as she walked up the road. She wouldn't judge Arlene even though this disaster must be of her own doing. She would talk to her on the phone and hope that she was calmer now and could give a few answers to the questions she needed to ask.

Ellie was still there when she arrived, placing some house details in an envelope and licking down the flap.

'Well, m'dear,' she said as she saw Cara. 'There's been trouble here today.'

Cara looked at her in surprise. She had forgotten that she had removed the painting and hidden it in Bal Cottage. But it seemed of trivial importance now. 'Yes, I've got it,' she said. 'It's at Bal Cottage.'

It was Ellie's turn to look surprised.

'You're talking about the painting?' asked Cara.

'Painting? No. It's Mark. Rushed to hospital this afternoon. Appendicitis. He came in for a while first thing to see a client, almost doubled up, but I sent him home at once.' 'He'll be OK?'

'Josh phoned. Mark's had the operation. He's back in the ward. He's going to be all right. A shock though. Josh will have to help out here. He won't like that. He's got a lot on.'

Cara saw that Ellie looked pale. 'Go off home, why don't you?' she said.

The phone rang. Ellie picked up the receiver. 'For you,' she said, handing it to Cara.

'An emergency,' Cara said. 'I said my sister could ring me here.'

Ellie nodded abstractedly as she gathered her handbag and buttoned the front of her cardigan.

Arlene's voice sounded firmer this evening but it still had that edge of desperation that had been in it earlier. 'It's a man,' she said. 'I lent him money, you see. A lot, from our joint account. And my credit cards . . . And now we can't pay the mortgage . . . '

'A man?' This was worse than Cara had thought. 'But why . . . ?'

'He needed it for his business. And now it's gone bankrupt. There's a bookies near here. I tried to win some money. He knows about horses, you see.'

'But not enough,' said Cara grimly. She bit the tip of her tongue to prevent herself saying more. She had had no idea things were this bad. She glanced round the office. 'Do you want me to come up?'

'I need the money. You do see?'

'I'll get my savings out tomorrow. That'll help you in the interim?'

A sob on the other end of the phone was the only answer.

'But Arlene, you've got to tell Tom. I'll get to the building society as soon as they open and drive up straight away. We need to sort this out between us. But you must tell Tom. I won't come otherwise. Promise me.'

There was low gurgling murmuring on the other end of the phone and Cara had to be content with that.

* * *

Cara awoke as light was beginning to strengthen outside her bedroom window. She lay for a moment, feeling a strange lethargy. Arlene's problem was a huge weight pressing her down.

She wished the building society opened this early so that she could arrange for a cheque to be made out to Arlene for the full amount of her savings right away. After that she would drive straight to Exeter and hand it over personally.

She must hear exactly how the position lay and how Tom would deal with it. She knew that if there was nothing else to be done they would sell the cottage.

A moment's doubt made her pause. Suppose Josh had only been saying that, a ruse to get them on their books? A cold shiver ran down her spine. But they would deal with that when they came to it.

She packed a few things in her bag and carried it downstairs. A cold drink and a biscuit from the tin was all she could manage. Then she let herself out of the front door and walked a short way up the road to where she could lean on the railings and look down at the harbour. When she turned her head she could see Bal Cottage to her right.

This moment was the lowest she had experienced. She told herself that she should be grateful for having had the chance to live and work here even for so short a time.

She should be glad she had learnt a little about her grandparents and she would always have that knowledge. She would have the memory of discovering the pebble vortex on the bank in the back garden. But it was not enough, could never be enough.

She felt a presence beside her, knowing it was Josh but unable to see him properly for the tears in her eyes.

'Cara,' he said, his voice gentle.

She looked away from him and saw that the strengthening sunlight had highlighted the top of Bal Cottage's thatched roof so that it looked as if someone had painted a distorted golden line there. It was beautiful.

Putting her head on her arms she

wept, not caring that Josh was standing there seeing her in a state of utter dejection. He remained still, making no attempt to touch her, until her tears were exhausted.

She raised her swollen eyes and stared down at the grey water down below. 'Arlene's in trouble,' she said with a catch in her voice. 'I've got to help.'

'Bad trouble?'

She nodded, rubbing her hand across her wet face. 'I didn't know it was so desperate . . . debt, gambling and worse, I think. I don't know it all . . . ' She felt tears threaten again and took a deep breath to calm herself.

'What of her husband?'

'I don't know. Tom's a good man but . . . And there are the children. I can't stay living here when . . . And I'd found some wood, old wood. I want to look at my grandfather's book again and see if . . . But there won't be time now. The vortex,' she sobbed. 'They'll dig it up and I'll never be able to finish it.'

'When did you find this wood? Was it recently?'

She nodded, sniffing and feeling for a tissue in her pocket. 'Yesterday after Arlene phoned. She said . . . There's nothing for it. We'll have to sell the cottage. It's got to be quick, you see. We need to get the money at once.' She sniffed again. But how likely was that to happen? Even with an immediate purchaser it would take weeks to go through. It was hopeless.

Josh threw his head back and as she looked at him she knew this was the end. She wouldn't see him again because she couldn't bear to stay in Polmerrick with someone else living in her grandparents' home. She put her head down on her hands once more. 'And there won't be time to go back and paint on that hidden beach, the next one where I found the waterlogged wood when the tide was low,' she muttered.

When she raised her head again he had gone. The wood was important to him, she thought, the discovering of old shipwrecks whose timbers had lain forgotten for years beneath the sea. She had done that for him at least.

Calmer now and feeling a new strength she returned to Bal Cottage and looked at it as if seeing it for the first time. The sun had risen above the hill on the other side of the harbour and bathed the cottage in a pink glow. Someone else would love it as she loved it.

She would find somewhere else to live and paint. Her life would go on. It was time now to think of her family, her sister, Arlene, whose desperate plight could be alleviated in some measure with her share of the proceeds of the cottage. Their inheritance had helped her work out a new life for herself and now it must do the same for Arlene.

She smelt the salt in the air mingled with the hint of wood smoke and knew she would remember this and carry it as a memory for the rest of her life. With her head high she went inside to make her final preparations for the visit to the building society in town and then to start her journey to Exeter.

9

'You'd do this for me?' Arlene looked at Cara, her eyes red-rimmed. Her brown hair, usually so luxuriant, hung in limp strands round her face.

Cara nodded. They were in the front room of the house in Exeter and Tom, her brother-in-law, stood at the window gazing out at the small front garden as if he had never seen it before. The slump of his shoulders showed his hurt on the disgrace his wife had brought to the family.

Cara was glad that the children were spending time with his mother on the other side of the city, knowing nothing of this. 'Yes, of course, I agree to Bal Cottage going on the market,' she said firmly.

Tom spun round. 'It's asking a lot of you, Cara.'

She nodded again. 'I'll do it. I'll get

back there today and get things moving first thing in the morning. You'd like me to make all the decisions about the sale, Arlene?'

Her sister shrugged. 'Please make it soon. I don't know what will happen if . . . '

Tom came to her and put his arm round his wife. 'We're dealing with it together, Arlene love. With the property to sell there'll be a breathing space. If we're lucky. Stay the night, Cara. It's not going to make a lot of difference.'

Cara smiled to see them together. What had happened between them before she arrived she didn't know, but it looked as if Tom was going to support Arlene as best he could and she was glad.

The three of them had spent all afternoon discussing the means of solving most of the problem . . . the selling of Bal Cottage.

Cara had struggled to keep from showing in any way all this meant to her, but knew she wasn't entirely successful, especially with the newly-humbled Arlene. But it seemed to bring them closer together, somehow, closer than they had been for years.

That this had come out of it helped to alleviate Cara's pain a little. Now she just wanted to get things sorted out without delay. Since it had to happen she wanted it to happen fast.

She yawned. It had been a long day. She banished from her mind how it had started when Josh had come upon her in her anguish as she stood at the railings. She didn't want to think of Josh in the midst of all this.

All the way to Polmerrick next morning she mused on the way things had turned out.

She wished she had known at the beginning how things would be and then she might have been satisfied with her three-week holiday in Polmerrick and not hankered for more.

This morning she had left Arlene looking more hopeful. Tom had taken the rest of the week off to be with her and to help get their lives back together again.

Cara hoped that soon she would be able to report that things were moving to their advantage in Polmerrick and that people were interested and making offers on their property. And that everything was going through without any fuss. She felt she deserved that they should as she hastened towards what had to be done.

A fire engine's intrusive bell invaded her thoughts. She pulled over to let it pass and waited while another roared past after it. Even then, seeing both turn off for Polmerrick, it didn't dawn on her that there was any seriousness in what she was seeing. Afterwards she wondered at her calm that was like a glass wall separating her from reality.

She drove down the road. At the bottom, near the post office, the police roadblock stopped her. She could see the smoke, smell the burning of the warehouse next to Bal Cottage, hear the shouts and the crackle of wood. She was conscious of people near her, Ellie Trevean and the woman from the shop. Eric Trubshaw and several workmen from the small factory outlet from up the road not far away.

'Oh my dear life!' cried Ellie in dismay. 'Bal Cottage'll be next.'

'The roof's been doused,' one of the men shouted.

Streams of water arched above the cottage but nothing, it seemed, could stop the angry flames darting from one building to the other.

'Look, the thatch has caught,' Ellie sobbed.

In horror, Cara watched the licking flames run along the top of the roof where this morning she had seen the golden line the sun had made. She tried to strain forward, but was held by strong restraining hands. Tristan.

She hardly recognised him through a blur of pain. It was a nightmare situation and she could do nothing except sniff in this choking smell of burning.

Part of the cottage roof had caved in now. It looked like more would follow, but the hoses seemed gradually to be doing their work. Most of the warehouse had collapsed and acrid fumes from its smoking contents stung Cara's eyes. A pall of black smoke filled the air.

And still the hoses directed water on the cottage. Surely the contents would have gone by now, the bedrooms walls crumbled? Tears ran down Cara's cheeks but she made no effort to control them.

'It'll be hours yet before anyone can get anywhere near,' someone told them.

'You'd best come home with me,' Ellie said. 'The shops are all shutting and the Miners' Rest'll not open. Polmerrick will be a dead place tonight. You've had a shock, m'dear. We all have, but none so much as you.'

'I'll tell the police where to find you,' Tristan said gruffly. His arm was round her still though he was aiming his video camera with the other.

She wondered why he was doing this

and then remembered his newspaper. This was not only a personal tragedy. This was news. She took a long sobering breath.

'Where's Josh?' said Ellie. 'He was here not long since.'

Cara's legs were beginning to give out and she was glad to let Ellie take over.

'Go, my love,' said Tristan, relinquishing her. 'I'll come when I can.'

★   ★   ★

Cara wouldn't think, couldn't work out what was best to do. They wouldn't allow her in to Bal Cottage, of course. From Ellie's small flat she would be able to phone Exeter and tell Arlene and Tom.

Any hope of a quick return on the cottage had gone. She had to let them know at once.

Ellie's flat was near the top of the road out of Polmerrick so there was no problem about getting there. Although the flames had gone from down on the harbour side and the fire seemed to be out, smoke still hung over it all. It would be ages yet before anyone could get near.

'We'll hear the fire engines go,' said Ellie as she unlocked her door and ushered Cara inside. 'And the police and all of them.'

'Can I use your phone, Ellie?' Cara asked.

'Over there, m'dear. I'll just get the kettle on.'

Arlene and Tom would be shattered. Cara knew that if she didn't phone at once she would put it off and the message she had to convey would seem even worse. She put down the receiver after the worst phone call of her life, feeling ill. She didn't care if she ate ever again or had a bed to sleep in.

Ellie made tea and produced cheese sandwiches. The lines on her face had deepened and her hands trembled a little. 'I'm worried about Josh,' she said. 'He was away today on some business of his own. Promised to get back about four and take on some of Mark's clients.'

Cara stared at her blankly. It seemed eons of years ago that Ellie had told her about Mark's operation.

The phone rang. Ellie sprang to answer it, her grey hair escaping from the knot at the back of her neck. Cara could hear the relief in her voice as she spoke. 'He's coming here,' she said to Cara.

In less than five minutes Josh was at the door. His hands and face were blackened and his jacket had a couple of buttons missing and a huge jagged tear in the right sleeve. 'I had to check,' he said hoarsely.

'There, there, boy, see for yourself,' Ellie said soothingly, ushering him inside.

Cara was shocked at his appearance. He took one look at her and collapsed into an easy chair, stretching his long legs in front of him. 'Where were you?' he demanded.

'Let me have that jacket,' Ellie said.

He shrugged himself out of it, not taking his eyes from Cara's face. She could see a scratch on his wrist and some congealed blood. With the jacket over her arm Ellie left the room muttering about finding more buttons and what on earth was he thinking of to get himself into such a state.

'I've been to see my sister,' Cara said quietly.

'You weren't in the cottage?'

She shook her head and saw that the colour in his face came and went. He closed his eyes. It seemed as if she was seeing his face for the first time, loving the tiny lines that edged the corners of his eyes and the way his dark hair fell over his forehead.

'And is it as you thought?' he murmured.

She nodded and then realised he wasn't looking at her. 'It would have been if . . .'

'We need to talk. Tomorrow.' He opened his eyes and looked vaguely round the room as if wondering how he had got here. 'Tomorrow will make more sense.'

★ ★ ★

Nine o'clock was striking on Ellie's sitting-room clock when Cara woke in the spare bedroom the next day. She lay still for a moment, staring at the unfamiliar flowery curtains.

A tap on the door roused her and she was sitting up and about to get out of bed when Ellie came in bearing a tray. She placed it carefully on the table beside the bed. 'I thought you could do with a cup of tea, m'dear,' she said.

'You're so kind,' said Cara gratefully.

'Now take your time getting up. There's no hurry. The police called in, but I said you were sleeping. They'll come back. Someone will deal with things for you if you're in no fit state. When you're ready I'll walk down with you. It's all cordoned off, of course, and you won't be allowed inside yet, but

157

you'll want to see it.'

'Shouldn't you be in the office, Ellie?' Cara asked as she reached for her tea.

Ellie pulled back the curtains and turned to smile at her. 'We'll open late today, m'dear. Don't you worry your head about that. I'll leave you to it then.'

Still feeling dazed after the events of yesterday, Cara got up slowly. Nothing seemed to matter any more. She packed her belongings in the overnight bag she'd had with her in Exeter and went to find Ellie. To her surprise she felt hungry and was glad of the cereal and toast Ellie had ready for her.

Together they drove in Cara's car down the road to the harbour. Cara had prepared herself for the shock of seeing where the fire had raged, but the reality was still unexpected because she hadn't seen anything like this before. The warehouse next door was now a shell, all the wood stored in there completely gone.

Bal Cottage was a shambles of how it

had been before. The walls were there and some of the roof, but it looked desecrated and forlorn. Cara stared at it, feeling nothing, hardly aware of the smell that lingered on the quiet air.

Ellie was talking to the man guarding the property. She came back to Cara and laid a hand on her arm. 'He says they've got to check it's safe to go in before they allow anyone near,' she said. 'Come back later, m'dear. They'll know what's what then, I shouldn't wonder.'

Cara nodded and took a long last look at the cottage that had become her home.

She hadn't expected Arlene and Tom to come, though of course they should be here. She was grateful for Tom's presence because she was still weak with shock and could hardly take in what had to be done.

They found her in Pellew's office doing some cleaning of the back rooms that she had neglected yesterday. The Miners' Rest was open today and she took them there to lunch at Ellie's suggestion.

Afterwards they went as close to the cordoned off area as they could and in silence looked at what was left of their inheritance.

Tom was the first to speak. 'I don't think we shall do any good here. We need to talk to someone, find out what's going on.' He glanced at his watch. 'It's going to be a slow job. Why don't you girls go off and get a coffee somewhere while I find someone? And then I think we should see the solicitor.'

It seemed a good idea. Tom was always a man of action. He would find this waiting about irksome in the extreme.

'Right, we'll leave him to it,' said Arlene. 'Where shall we go?'

'Tell you what,' said Tom. 'I'll meet you in town in about half-an-hour. I've got your solicitor's number. I'll arrange an appointment and get back to you on your mobile, Arlene.'

'Wait a minute,' said Cara. 'Why? I mean . . . '

'I suggest we arrange for the solicitor to sort out the insurance for us. By far the best way. It could be complicated. It'll take months anyway, so the sooner we start the better. We'll need to get estimates for the rebuilding, the re-thatching . . . '

Cara leaned back against a fence post and looked at him in dismay. She wasn't ready for this yet. 'I don't think . . . '

'We'll have to get off back home quickly after that to pick up the children,' Tom said, not registering her hesitation.

'I'll stay in Polmerrick,' said Cara. Ellie had invited her to stay at her flat and that's what she would be doing for the time being.

He looked at her in surprise. 'D'you want me to do that side of it with Arlene then?'

'I think it's best,' said Cara weakly. 'I'm not feeling too good, Tom. I'd rather leave it for a while. But if you think . . . '

'Right then. I'll pick you up outside the Miners' Rest in say, three quarters of an hour, Arlene. All right? We'll say goodbye then, Cara. We'll phone later with any information.'

Cara was glad to stay sitting outside in the sunshine for a little while after they had gone. She hadn't reminded them that she got no signal from the cottage, but of course, that didn't apply now. Maybe she could from Ellie's. In any case, she was too tired to care. She still felt shocked at what had happened and needed to be close to Bal Cottage for her own sake.

By late afternoon she wandered down the road towards the cottage and found that the cordon had been moved further back, close to the cottage walls. 'I want to go into the back garden,' she told the man still on duty. 'I'll be careful, but there's something I want to see.'

He was obviously getting ready to leave. There were warning notices everywhere and she wasn't going to ignore them.

The fire-fighters had trodden every-where as they did their job, trampling down the remaining brambles. Ladders had been erected, churning up the earth. Cara looked in dismay at the strewn pebbles that had once been the vortex pattern. They were everywhere. The work so longingly done all those years ago was no more.

She threw herself down on the damp ground and grabbed together as many as she could into a rough pile though what she would do with them she didn't know. The centre of the vortex was ruined completely. She couldn't bear it.

This was her lowest ebb yet as she stared disbelievingly at the desecration. She had thought that yesterday was bad when she stood weeping at the railing with Josh. But that was nothing to this.

She wasn't aware of the passing time, only of the need to rebuild the work her grandparents had done. But she couldn't do it now, not now. Tomorrow. Yes, early tomorrow she would return and set to work even if she made a total mess of it.

She had time to return to Ellie's place and change back into the skirt she had worn yesterday. She placed her muddy jeans over the back of a chair and then hurried down the road to Pellew's. Shocked she might be, but she had the wits to know that's where she should be at this time of day.

Ellie was there when she arrived, working late to make up for the late start this morning. Two clients, a man and a woman were seated in front of her desk examining some brochures with a great deal of interest.

Cara went to the cupboard in the passageway, deciding to make a start on the back premises first. She was glad of the dimness after the glare of sunshine outside. She needed it at the moment. She leaned her head against the cupboard door, knowing she must make the effort to act normally and not to go over and over in her mind the harrowing thoughts that filled it.

She heard the clients leave and Ellie lock the front entrance behind them.

There were a few moments when Ellie was obviously gathering her things together and then she came to find Cara.

'Leave that, m'dear,' she said kindly. 'Come through into the office and I'll get the kettle on. It's clean enough in here for today and you've got other things to think about. You look as white as the paper on my desk. Apart from the one with writing on, of course,' she added. 'And that's one you might like to see.'

Cara did as she said and sat down in one of the vacated chairs by the desk. She took the paper Ellie handed to her and looked at it, frowning. It was a jumble of senseless words. She looked appealingly at Ellie. 'But what is it?' she asked.

'What is it?' said Ellie in surprise. 'It's an offer on Bal Cottage, m'dear. It came through on the fax machine not ten minutes before you came in.'

10

Cara gazed down at the paper. This was Josh's doing. She was sure of it. The offer was low, too low. No-one in her right mind would accept this.

She crushed the paper in her hand and thrust it into the pocket of her denim skirt, simply not caring about any of it. Let the others do what they would. She was no longer interested.

She felt the crackle of the paper as she walked by Ellie's side back to her place. Tristan, his face pale and anxious, was at the door.

'Cara!' he said. 'You're all right?'

'She's tired,' said Ellie sharply. 'Tomorrow maybe.'

'I had to come now. I couldn't make it last night.'

Cara tried to smile, pleased to see him but exhausted too. 'Thanks, Tristan.'

'You saw your painting in the window?'

She looked at him blankly. What was he talking about?

'In Pellews' window?'

'You put it there? But why?'

He looked pleased with himself. 'For somebody to buy, of course, at the full price, all to be handed to you, my love. I knew you'd paint me a replacement.'

Cara felt that her head was reeling with the implications of what he said. Josh wasn't to blame at all. It had been an odd accident that the holiday property advertisement had been near it.

'You're a good friend,' she said weakly.

'More than that I hope.'

'No,' she said. 'Not more. Please, I must go . . . ' She knew he was hurt, but could do nothing about it.

Ellie, looking fussed, already had the door open and Cara went thankfully inside.

The crumpled paper was still in her

pocket when Cara set out for Bal Cottage. Ellie had put her jeans in the wash as soon as she could get hold of them. With luck she would be allowed into Bal Cottage before long to check through the wreckage and discover what remained of her belongings as well as the state of the rest of the contents.

Even though she knew the pebble vortex was nearly destroyed it was a shock to see the pile of pebbles she had amassed yesterday heaped on the black earth. She knelt down beside it.

The centre of the vortex was the most dangerous and beneath the discarded pebbles she saw raw earth that no-one had seen for many years. She put her hand down to pat it and to her surprise felt the earth fall away until she was looking down a hole the size of a football. There was something inside, something wrapped in some sort of black waterproof material. She edged it out, brushed off the damp soil and opened it.

Inside was a book, its brown covers

dark with age and sprinkled with mould. Was this another book written by her grandfather about shipwrecks along the coast?

Carefully she opened it and saw faint spidery handwriting. Colour flooded her face as she realised what this was. The name on the first page was familiar because the curator at the museum had told her. Marion Karrivick, her grandmother. This was a series of written notes . . . a record of some important events in her life. The first was a description of Bal Cottage on the day they had moved in.

In mounting excitement Cara started to read it, but then she closed the book. She needed to take it slowly, to savour every word, and she needed to do that where she wouldn't be disturbed. She checked inside the hole again. Nothing else there but she had to be sure.

Standing up, she pushed earth back with one foot to disguise it. Then, with the precious book held protectively against her, she left the garden of Bal

Cottage and made for the cliff path. She didn't look back at the empty plot where the warehouse used to be or at her damaged cottage. She kept going until she reached the steep and narrow path that lead down to the secluded beach she had found the other day. Here she could study the book undisturbed.

It was a happy story at first, soon to turn to sadness as the deaths of her son and daughter-in-law were recorded. Before that Marion had written about the birth of the twins, her grandchildren, Cara and Arlene. She and their grandfather had been so proud.

The lump in Cara's throat was painful as she read the story of loss that followed. It seemed that the writing of it was too sad to be continued. Was it then that Marion had buried the book in the garden and constructed the pebble vortex above?

It seemed very much as if she had. And now the book was found when the children were grown up. A message from the past. Cara found that tears were rolling down her cheeks as she came to the end of the handwritten entries. She let them flow, careful not to let them fall on the page, knowing that they were tears of healing.

After a while she closed the book and laid it to one side. She noticed for the first time that the day was lovely with tiny white clouds moving across a sky so blue it seemed unreal. She lay on her back gazing up at it, the sunshine drying her face, and listened to the waves breaking on the sand and the call of sea birds in the distance.

She closed her eyes, letting her grandmother's words wash over her, calming her.

She must have slept because when she sat up she saw that there were rocks where there hadn't been before and that the line of rippling waves was farther away. She rubbed her eyes, yawning. A small boat had come in and lay empty on its side on the wet sand at one side of the cove.

Drowsily, she wondered who had left it there and if she had been noticed lying here asleep. Then she saw a figure seated on the rocks, almost indiscernible against the darkness of the cliffs. Josh, of course.

He got up and strode across the soft sand towards her. 'I was looking for you,' he said. He sat down beside her.

'I found this,' she said, handing him the book.

He opened it, head bowed. She felt the warmth of his body and was glad he had come. His white T-shirt was stained across his back as he leaned forward to read. He took a long time. 'I see,' he said at last, still looking down at the last page. He turned to the beginning and studied her grandmother's signature with concentration almost as if he was willing it to tell him more.

Cara let out a small sigh, knowing that there was no longer any need to explain to him how it had been, that she and Arlene hadn't known their grandparents through no fault of their own. Somehow he knew this without any telling and the knowledge of that warmed her.

He would not then have condemned her, but that was her fault for allowing him to believe what he wanted. She lifted a handful of sand and let it run through her fingers. She had no pride left now where Josh was concerned and the relief was enormous.

At last he closed the book and returned it to her.

'They'll never know we came back,' she said sadly. 'It's all too late. I know that my grandfather was sad and lonely when we could have been here for him, for both of them.'

'But you've come to Polmerrick now,' he said gently. 'You've found something that links you with them. No-one can take this from you, Cara.'

She nodded. This was true and she was glad of it. 'Why did you come here?' she asked. 'Was it for the blackened wood?'

'Blackened wood?' He stared at her

uncomprehendingly.

'I thought it might be from an old shipwreck,' she explained.

His face cleared. 'Oh that. I reported that when you told me. It was dealt with at once.'

'So why, then?'

'No-one knew where you were.' He shivered. 'Like yesterday. I didn't know then either.'

She looked at him, suddenly realising why he was in such a filthy state when he turned up at Ellie's cottage.

'You were looking for me yesterday too?' she said in surprise.

He shrugged. 'I had to be sure you weren't in the cottage.'

'I was with my sister.'

He nodded. 'Did you get my fax?'

Involuntarily her hand flew to her pocket. She pulled out the crumpled paper and smoothed it out. 'This?' Has he come looking for her merely for this? All he wanted from her was to know if she would sell Bal Cottage to him for this ridiculously insulting price. That was all. She leapt up.

'What's wrong?' he said, springing up too.

She didn't want him to see how hurt she was. She set off across the sand, her back held straight.

'Hey, wait a minute!'

He caught up with her as she reached the path. Grabbing hold of her, he pulled her round to face him.

'Let me go!'

'Not until you see sense.'

'What sense is there to see?'

His face, close to hers, flushed. 'Someone from up country looking for investment will buy it ... some uncaring person buying it cheap to do it up with their way-out ideas, tarted up to sell on and make a huge profit? Do you want that for your grandparents' home ... do you? Tell me, is that what you want?'

She flinched. 'No!'

'Then consider my offer. I've enough for half the present value of the cottage. I spent the day before yesterday sorting out my finances, making my funds easily available. I'm collecting Mark from hospital this afternoon. He can deal with it, see your solicitor about the sale on your behalf and get it all tied up legally. He'll be glad of something to do. You and I will be busy with other things like sorting out the cottage.'

'You said half the present value?'

'To go with your half, my love.' He released her but steadied her as he did so, holding on to her hand. 'I want to be in your life and you in mine.'

She looked at him as he stood there with the sun shining on his fair hair and knew he meant it. He pulled her to him and bent his head so that she felt his warm breath on her face. His kiss was long and hard and when he let her go she was breathless.

But still she hesitated.

He seemed to understand why. The expression in his eyes was tender as he cupped her chin in his hand. 'Listen, my beautiful one. Arlene will have her share of the insurance money in due course. And she'll have the money I'm offering at once. This will surely be enough for her immediate needs.'

'It will with the money I've lent her,' Cara said wonderingly. Arlene would be all right. She would too, with half a damaged cottage that would take months to rebuild and be habitable again. But this was Bal Cottage and important to her and Josh knew this. His offer was more than reasonable for Arlene's half of the cottage.

'I never did get the front door key cut,' she said.

He smiled. 'We'll sort all that out together. So what do you say, my love?'

What could she say? It was hard to take in with Josh looking at her so intently as if his whole life depended on her answer. She bent down and picked up a pebble, smoothing it with her fingers. 'I'd better start collecting pebbles,' she said in an explanation that sounded odd.

'Thank goodness for that,' Josh said, smiling in obvious relief. 'Bal Cottage would be no good to me without the pebble vortex complete. That's what it's all about, isn't it, making it good again to be the perfect place for your workshop and gallery? There's hard work ahead of us.'

She gave a little trembling laugh and was at once folded in his arms again. This time his kiss was long and lingering. The atmosphere was charged, suddenly, with a shaft of such beauty she pulled away and looked at him in wonder. The loving expression in his eyes was almost too much to bear.

He pulled her towards him again and she almost melted into his arms this time as he kissed her. He laughed as he let her go again and she laughed too, brushing her loose hair away from her face.

She plunged her hand in her pocket and found the perfect smoothness of the pebble. Pulling it out she handed it to him. 'Yours,' she said, a tremor in her voice. 'This will be the last pebble for you to fit into its proper place.'

He took it from her. 'Isn't this where I came in?' he said.

'And will stay,' she said happily.

THE END

We do hope that you have enjoyed reading this large print book.

Did you know that all of our titles are available for purchase?

We publish a wide range of high quality large print books including:
**Romances, Mysteries, Classics
General Fiction
Non Fiction and Westerns**

Special interest titles available in large print are:
**The Little Oxford Dictionary
Music Book, Song Book
Hymn Book, Service Book**

Also available from us courtesy of Oxford University Press:
**Young Readers' Dictionary
(large print edition)
Young Readers' Thesaurus
(large print edition)**

For further information or a free brochure, please contact us at:
**Ulverscroft Large Print Books Ltd.,
The Green, Bradgate Road, Anstey,
Leicester, LE7 7FU, England.
Tel:** (00 44) **0116 236 4325**
Fax: (00 44) **0116 234 0205**

Other titles in the
Linford Romance Library:

IN A WELSH VALLEY

Catriona McCuaig

When Ruth Greene's cousin Dora has to go into hospital, Ruth's family rallies round by going to look after the grocery shop she runs in her Welsh mining village in Carmarthenshire. This gives them a respite from the London blitz, but other dangers and excitements await them in their temporary home. Young Basil gets into mischief, while their daughter, Marina, falls in love for the first time. But can her wartime love endure?

MILLION DOLLAR DREAM

Joanna Hunt

Giorgi had secretly adored Rafe all her life, but he was madly in love with — and destined to marry — her sister, Anna. But when Anna died, their fathers' dream to unite the two families and their wineries was thwarted . . . Will Giorgi marry Rafe, give up her city restaurant and return to the Australian Sunset company as his wife, knowing he doesn't love her? Or will she retain her independence, and deny any chance she may have had of happiness with him?

A COUNTRY MOUSE

Fenella Miller

Emily Gibson is a spirited young woman who wishes to make her own way in life. She has been looking after her family since her father died, but with mounting debts something must be done. Deciding that she must marry for money, she writes to ask her estranged grandfather, the Earl of Westerham, to put forward an appropriate suitor. But he selects her cousin — and he's the last person Emily would have chosen. Can love blossom in such circumstances?

MISS GEORGINA'S CURE

Valerie Holmes

When Georgina's path crosses with that of William Philip Carter's horse, her life takes a dramatic and unexpected turn for the better. The affluent and mysterious Mr Carter placates her anxious mother and takes both of them into his manor house. Unwittingly, he is forced to face dark shadows from his own past. He has rescued Georgina from life with her impoverished family, the result of selfish and weak menfolk: an act which will change his own world forever . . .

BITTER HARVEST

Catriona McCuaig

When she learns that her partner is not only unfaithful, but is also a confidence trickster, Michaela Clarke believes that she can never trust a man again. While struggling to come to terms with what has happened to her she meets handsome Jerome Marshall. While instantly attracted to him, she is wary of becoming involved again, especially as he comes from an enormously wealthy family. Can love find a way?

SO NEAR TO LOVE

Gillian Kaye

Despite Emma's dislike of Mr Peirstone, schoolmaster in Ellerdale, she is forced to go to School House to look after his children. There she meets his son, Adam, and falls in love. But Adam's circumstances don't allow for marriage. Then Mr Peirstone dies unexpectedly and Emma goes to work for Dr Redman and his wife, Amy, in Ravendale. The doctor schemes to matchmake Emma and Adam . . . but can there ever be a happy ending for the young couple?